TANDEM

D0993362

15

Butcher of Belgrade

FOR SALE

TOP-SECRET NUCLEAR DEVICE. CONTACT TOPCON,
INC. BID ALREADY RECEIVED FROM U.S.S.R.

All Nick Carter knows is that one of America's top-
secret satellite devices is up for grabs. . . .

All Nick Carter knows is that the anonymous
mastermind of a private espionage syndicate called
Topcon, Inc., will personally conduct the auction. . . .

All Nick Carter knows is that the sale is to be made
aboard a high-speed express travelling across Europe,
and that the future of the U.S. hinges on the
outcome. . . .

All Nick Carter knows is that the train is crawling
with hired killers, double agents, and desperate
bidders . . . .

And that's all AXE agent Nick Carter needs to know
to plunge headlong into savage action and hair-raising
adventure!

Butcher of Belgrade

Nick Carter

TANDEM
14 Gloucester Road, London, SW7

Originally published in the United States
by Univesal-Award House, Inc., 1973

First published in Great Britain by Universal-Tandem
Publishing Co. Ltd., 1974

Dedicated to
The Men of the Secret Services
of the
United States of America

Made and printed in Great Britain by
Hunt Barnard Printing Ltd., Aylesbury, Bucks.

BUTCHER OF BELGRADE

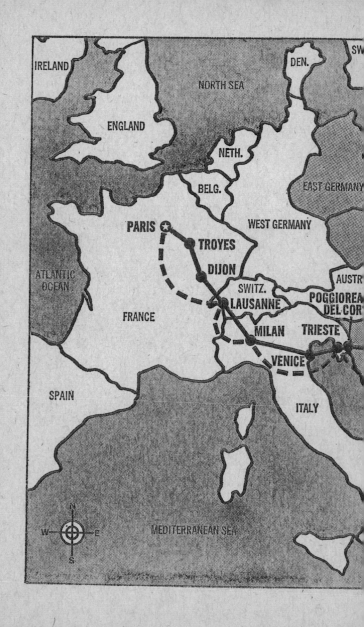

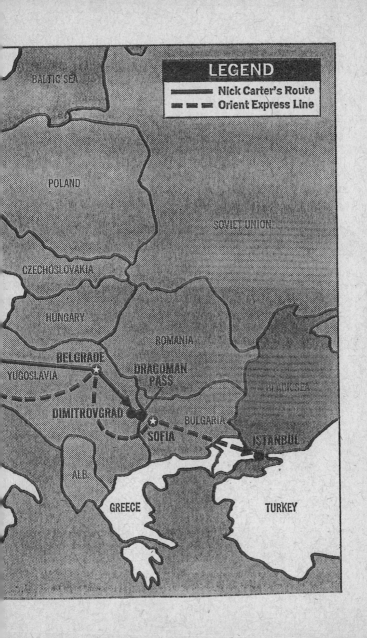

LEGEND
— Nick Carter's Route
- - - Orient Express Line

BALTIC SEA

POLAND

SOVIET UNION

CZECHOSLOVAKIA

HUNGARY

ROMANIA

BELGRADE
YUGOSLAVIA

DRAGOMAN
PASS

BLACK SEA

DIMITROVGRAD

SOFIA

BULGARIA

ISTANBUL

ALB.

GREECE

TURKEY

Prologue

Like a great black snake, the Orient Express slid out of the station at Milan. Picking up speed, the train burst out of the city and into the green Italian countryside, whining along the rails as it raced toward Trieste.

In a compartment near the rear of the swaying train, a small, nervous man sat alone, his brown suitcase at his feet. His name was Carlo Spinetti. He was a tradesman, homeward bound after a journey to visit distant relatives. As he gazed out of the train window at the landscape speeding past, he thought how glad he would be to see his wife and children again. This business of travel might be exciting for some, but for Carlo Spinetti the incessant hustle and bustle of crowds proved a strain on the nerves.

A tall man opened the door to the compartment and stood looking at Carlo with cool, dark eyes that seemed to have been chiseled out of ebony. His gaze dropped to the brown suitcase Carlo had not bothered to place in the luggage rack. A faint smile curled the corner of the man's mouth, and then he stepped the rest of

7

the way into the compartment and sat down opposite Carlo, stretching his long legs out in front of him.

"Getting off at Trieste, are you?" he asked.

Carlo Spinetti blinked and stirred in his seat. He was surprised that this stranger knew his destination. He said, "Yes, and you?"

The man continued to smile as though he knew about a joke that was being kept from Carlo. "I am also getting off at Trieste."

Five minutes later, a heavyset man entered the compartment. He closed the door and leaned against it, studying Spinetti as the first man had. His gaze, too, dropped to the bag at Spinetti's feet. Then he nodded to the tall man as though the two of them knew each other from some distant past.

Instinctively, Carlo reached down and shifted the suitcase that seemed to interest the two strangers. He could not have explained their interest. The bag was battered and worn, and it contained little of value except Carlo's clothing and some small gifts he was taking home to his family.

"Are you going to Trieste too?" he nervously inquired of the second stranger.

"Yes." The voice was gruff and harsh. The heavyset man sank to a seat alongside the first stranger and folded his arms over his chest. He sat there silently, his eyes hooded as though he had dozed off, while the train churned on.

Carlo wriggled uncomfortably. He told himself he must be imagining the threat he felt behind their casual words. Both men were more expensively dressed than he was. Their faces appeared hard, but they did not look like thieves who stole from innocent travelers.

"What is the matter with you, my friend? You seem a little jumpy," said the tall man mockingly.

Carlo worked a finger in his collar to loosen it. "I was wondering—could it be that you know me?"

"No, my friend, I don't know you."

"I have the feeling that you are staring at me."

"I'm looking at you, but I'm not staring," said the tall man. Then he laughed.

Carlo's nervousness was rapidly turning to fear. Telling himself that he didn't have to stay here, that he could change compartments, he leaned down and quickly grabbed hold of his suitcase. But as he started to move from his seat, the tall man across from him lashed out with his foot and pinned the suitcase in place, blocking Carlo's path with his leg.

"Do not leave us, my friend. We are enjoying your company," he said in a menacing voice.

Suddenly the eyes of the heavyset man flicked open. He glared at Carlo. "Yes, sit down. And be quiet if you don't want to be hurt."

Carlo dropped back into his seat. He was trembling. He felt something crawling on his cheek. He swiped at it with his hand, then realized it was a stream of sweat.

"Why are you doing this? I have never seen you before. What could you want from me?"

"I told you to be quiet," growled the heavyset man.

Bewildered and frightened, Carlo stayed in his seat until the train pulled into the station at Trieste. He was so terrified that he arose only when the heavyset man stood up and gestured. "Let's go. You walk ahead of us."

The tall man had reached into his coat. He produced a knife with a short, broad blade. "We will take your suitcase, my friend. Behave yourself if you wish to live."

Carlo protested. "I am carrying nothing of value in my suitcase. Surely this is a mistake; you have the wrong man."

"We have the right man and the right suitcase." The knife's sharp point pricked Carlo's neck. "Shut up and start walking."

As Carlo moved slowly down the steps of the train, sweating and shaking with fear, it came to him that perhaps these men would kill him no matter what he did. Panic thundered in his brain. He stepped to the station platform and his eyes caught a glimpse of a policeman's uniform in the crowd. Instinctively he yelled, "Please help me!"

He started to run toward the policeman, and then the blade of the knife sank savagely into his neck. He staggered, gasping. What was the reason for it? Why did they want his suitcase? Bewildered to the end, he lunged blindly off the edge of the platform and plunged downward onto the tracks with a scream that trailed off into a dying sob. . . .

One

A soft rain was falling on Washington. Thick fog hung over the city like a gray overcoat. When I looked from the window of my hotel room, I could see just about as far as I could throw the Pentagon. Just for the hell of it, I tried to make out the shape of the Soviet Embassy down the street. I wondered if any of the boys there were busy thinking up projects that I'd be assigned to abort.

The telephone rang and I moved to it quickly. I was waiting for a message from David Hawk, the man who called the signals for AXE, the cloak and dagger agency that employed me. The work was risky, and sometimes the hours were terrible, but I got to meet a lot of interesting people.

The voice that came over the line belonged to one of Hawk's assistants. "The Old Man is in a meeting and he sends word that he'll be tied up for quite a while. He says for you to take the night off and check in with him tomorrow."

"Thanks," I told the voice and hung up with a scowl. When David Hawk got tied up in long meetings, it usually meant something had gone wrong for our side.

Impatience gnawed at me as I stripped off my hardware—the Luger in the shoulder holster, the stiletto up my sleeve, the small gas bomb I often wore taped to the inside of my thigh—and stepped into the shower. Sometimes my business was just like the military: hurry up and wait. For two days now I'd been in Washington awaiting orders, and Hawk still hadn't told me what was up. When it came to inscrutability, many Orientals could have taken lessons from the lean-faced old pro who commanded AXE's operations.

Hawk had summoned me to the capital from New Delhi, where I'd just completed an assignment. The summons had been tagged Priority Two, which signified that urgent business was at hand. Only Priority One instructions could bring an agent winging homeward any faster, and Priority One was reserved for the kind of messages dispatched when the President was on the hot line and the Secretary of State was chewing his fingernails down to the knuckles.

Since my arrival, however, I'd been able to talk to Hawk only once, and that conversation had been brief. He'd told me only that he had an assignment coming up that was right down my alley.

Right down my alley. That probably meant it could get me killed.

I wound a towel around my waist and listened

to the news as I shaved. Now much was happening in the world that hadn't happened before, and most of that wasn't too good. Along with the dismal weather, it was enough to send a dedicated drinker back to the bar for another double bourbon. But it was not a night that couldn't be brightened up considerably if a man knew the right girl. And I knew one.

Her name was Ellen. She worked for one of those high-priced legal beagles who specialize in arguing cases before the Supreme Court. I didn't know how good an attorney he was, but if his briefs were one-half as dazzling as his secretary, he probably never lost a case.

I hadn't seen Ellen in almost a year, but since she knew the line of business I was in, I didn't have to offer any long-winded explanation when I called her. She said she'd cancel her other plans for the evening. I drove across town to her apartment in the car AXE had furnished for me. The fog was so thick I had to move at a snail's pace.

Ellen was wearing a clinging, low-cut black dress. She took my raincoat, then threw her arms around my neck, pressing her full breasts against me, and gave me a kiss that would have melted the eyebrows on a statue.

"You don't waste any time," I told her.

"With you, there's never any time to waste. You're here today, gone tomorrow." She smiled up at me. "I take it you're still working for that nasty old man, Hawk?"

"That's right, but tonight I'm all yours."

She raised an eyebrow. "That sounds very interesting, Mr. Carter."

We decided against going out. The weather was too lousy, and besides, the truth was that neither of us wanted to get too far away from the bedroom. After Ellen broiled us steaks as thick as the Sunday *New York Times,* we sat around and drank wine and talked about what had happened to us during the year since we'd seen each other. She brought me up to date on her activities, and I told her where I'd been, if not all of the things I'd done.

Then I put my glass down and moved closer to her on the long sofa. With a slow smile, she drained the rest of her wine and then leaned over, the black gown falling away from her white breasts, and placed her glass alongside mine.

"At last, Nick," she said. "I was beginning to think you'd never get around to it."

I laughed softly and let my fingers glide down into her gown and over the softness of her breast. Her nipple was hard and taut against my palm. I kissed her and felt her darting tongue, and then she turned and fell back into my lap.

Lingering on her mouth, I explored it until she was responding hotly. By the time the kiss was over, she was breathless, her breasts pumping up and down.

"Nick, it's been much too long."

It had indeed, I thought.

Rising, I pulled her to her feet, reached around and unfastened the dress in back. I slipped the straps slowly off her shoulders, then bared the full breasts. I kissed her again and her hands moved on my back.

"The bedroom where it used to be?" I asked.

She nodded, seeking my mouth again, and I picked her up and carried her through the door to the bed.

"All right?" I asked, standing over her as I peeled off my coat.

"All right, Nick."

I finished undressing and hung the Luger on the back of a chair. Ellen was watching me, her eyes dark and smoldering.

"I wish you hadn't worn that thing," she said. "It reminds me of what you do for a living."

"Someone has to do it."

"I know. But it's so dangerous. Come here, Nick. Hurry up. I want you now."

As I crossed to her, she was wriggling out of the dress and the black panties, which were all she wore underneath it. While I caressed her inner thigh, I placed a row of kisses across her breasts. She writhed as though my touch had set her afire.

Then I was entering her and she was surging

underneath me, timing her movements to mine. We climaxed together.

She was all that I had remembered, and more.

Our bodies were still joined when I heard the telephone on the bedside table ring. Ellen made a face, then wormed out from under me and picked up the receiver. She listened to the voice on the line, then thrust the receiver at me. "It's that man."

"I hope I didn't interrupt anything," said David Hawk.

"You came damn close," I told him. "How did you know where I was?"

"An educated guess, I suppose you'd call it. I know I told you to take the night off, Nick, but things have finally started to pop. I'd like for you to get over to the shop right now."

I slammed down the receiver, got out of bed, and put my clothes back on. "Any messages for that nasty old man?" I asked Ellen as I made my way to the door.

"Yes," she said with a faint smile. "Tell him I think his timing is terrific."

The rain had let up by the time I reached the Amalgamated Press and Wire Services Building, on Dupont Circle. This was the shop, as Hawk called it, the cover for AXE's center of operations.

Only the lights in Hawk's offices were burning as I hurried along the silent corridor. A pair of men sat in the outer office. One of them jerked his thumb toward the other door, and I went in and found Hawk at his desk. He looked as though he'd been missing too much sleep.

"Well, Nick, how was the night off?" he asked in a dry voice.

"It was great while it lasted." I sat down without being asked.

"I've been running from one damned meeting to another trying to get the details worked out on this assignment of yours." Hawk's contempt for red tape showed in his expression. "Now something has happened that lends it special urgency. I'm briefing you tonight because I want you on a plane to Paris in the morning."

"What do I do when I get there?"

Hawk opened a drawer and took out a manila folder. From the folder he extracted some photographs. He slid the pictures across the desk. "Look at these. That unimpressive little gadget you see there is an extremely valuable piece of equipment."

I examined the three photographs carefully. "It's an electronic device, obviously. But what else is it?"

"As you know, we have a very complex satellite monitoring system. It's much better than anything the Russians or the Chinese have been able to perfect. A great part of the success of our system is the gadget shown in those pictures. It has the capacity to zero in on a tiny moving target from a great distance, and to pick up the smallest sounds emitted by that target."

"I can see why it's valuable."

Hawk tore the wrapping off a black cigar. "It allows us to monitor everything the Soviets are receiving on their spy satellites, and to record it all for decoding later. As far as satellite intelligence is concerned, it's the most coveted item in the world."

"And it's no larger than a man's fist."

Hawk nodded and sank his teeth into the cigar. "Which means it's easy to steal and easy to conceal."

I could almost guess the rest. "Someone on the other side got hold of one of the devices?"

"We let the British have a few of them. One was stolen in London."

"The Russians?" I asked.

"No," Hawk said. "But they'd sure as hell like to have it. So would the Chinese. Now, let me ask you a question, Nick. How much do you know about an organization called Topcon?"

When I heard the name, I leaned forward. My reaction must have revealed my quickening interest because Hawk permitted himself a thin and somewhat weary smile.

"Topcon," I repeated. "I know that it exists. Like you, I hear the gossip of the spying trade."

"It's a privately owned and operated intelligence operation. An efficient one. It seemed to spring out of nowhere not long ago, but it immediately became a factor in the espionage war between East and West. Topcon steals secrets and sells them to the highest bidder. Up to now, it's been mostly our secrets that were stolen and mostly the Reds who bought them."

Hawk really was tired. He placed his unlighted cigar in an ashtray and knuckled his eyes. "Topcon is a shadowy organization, Nick, apparently tightly-knit and carefully policed. It may be the best private spying outfit set up since Gehlen formed his in Germany after the war. And we can't identify the person who heads it. That sort of information has eluded us."

"I know. I could make a couple of stops in almost any large city in Europe and come out with the addresses of the local Soviet and British intelligence chiefs, but Topcon is a different matter entirely. I couldn't give you the name of anyone who works for them."

"And I suppose you've been wondering when AXE would challenge this outfit and try to find out who runs it."

I grinned. "I'd like the job, if that's what you mean."

"Nick, Topcon has the precious little gadget shown in those photographs. They've put it up for auction."

Hawk opened the folder again and took out a newspaper clipping which he passed to me. "Before I go on, I want you to read this news item."

I frowned as I quickly scanned the clipping,

which was from an Italian language newspaper. The story was very brief. It reported the stabbing death of a traveler named Carlo Spinetti. The murder had been committed on a railroad platform in Trieste. Police were looking for two men who perpetrated the crime while stealing Carlo Spinetti's suitcase.

"What's the connection between this and the rest of what you've told me?" I asked Hawk.

"The killers weren't interested in the contents of their victim's suitcase. They wanted a travel sticker that was on the bag. A sticker that concealed a microdot with valuable intelligence on it." Hawk took the clipping back, shaking his head. "Carlo Spinetti wasn't even aware he was carrying it."

"Without his knowledge, he was being used to transport stolen data?"

"That's right. And Topcon was responsible. They're using the railroad to smuggle information, to carry stolen secrets out of the free world and behind the Iron Curtain. They use the Orient Express run from Paris to Sofia, by way of Milan, Trieste, and Belgrade. We've been watching the airways closely, so they developed another pipeline."

I was fitting the various bits of information together. "And you think the electronic device Topcon stole is going to be carried along that pipeline."

"Most of what I've told you comes to us from

a Bulgarian defector named Jan Skopje. He's informed us that Topcon has the gadget and plans to take it to Sofia aboard the Orient Express. One of Russia's people, a top KGB man, is scheduled to meet a Topcon agent aboard the train to make a deal before they arrive in Sofia. You, Nick, are to meet Skopje in Paris, pick up any other details you can, and intercept the merchandise before it changes hands."

I took another look at the photographs of the device. "Okay."

"I brought you to Washington with the intention of assigning you to locate the monitor. At that time, I didn't know who had it. Then the Skopje business started breaking, so I had to delay a decision."

"I understand. And now time is breathing down our necks. I have to get to the device before the Russians do."

"While you're doing that, if you should just happen to blow the lid off Topcon, I wouldn't be exactly unhappy."

"I'll see what I can arrange." I stood up. "Any further instructions?"

"You're going up against the KGB and Topcon. And Lord knows who else might horn in hoping to get hold of that monitor. So watch your step, Nick. I'd hate to lose both the monitor and you."

I promised that I'd try to save him that embarrassment.

Two

It was late afternoon of the next day when I arrived at Orly Airport near Paris. The weather was cool but clear, and the taxi ride to the Prince de Galles Hotel at 33, Avenue George V was very pleasant. Paris looked the same, except for the ever-burgeoning traffic on the streets. There were a few buds on the trees that lined the boulevards. I remembered some of my favorite streets with nostalgia: the Rue Réaumur with its iron-work balconies, the Montparnasse area, and the lovely Rue du Faubourg Poissonnière that led down to the Folies. But I had no time for any of that now. I had to find Jan Skopje.

By dark I was checked in at the Prince de Galles. I called Skopje at the number he had given us and reached him. His voice was deep with a thick accent and tense.

"Come to the Three Graces Square near the Folies," he told me. "At seven. The sooner the better, as you Americans say." There was a small nervous laugh. "I will be at Duke's Bar, just down the block from my hotel."

"I'll be there," I said.

Before I left the hotel, I checked the Luger I called Wilhelmina. I considered such precautions to be among the reasons I was still alive while a couple of Killmasters who had preceded me were listed as Cold War casualties in a special file Hawk kept in a locked drawer of his desk.

Testing the stiletto I called Hugo, I flexed my left arm. The deadly little knife slid neatly from the arm scabbard and down into my hand. I nodded to myself, satisfied that I was as prepared as I could be for what lay ahead, and then I went down the stairs and out into the spring sunlight.

I had an early dinner at the Chez des Anges Restaurant on the Boulevard de Latour-Maubourg coq au vin, oeufs en meurette, and a balloon glass of excellent Burgundy wine. Then I took a taxi to the Place de la République.

Because I knew the area and because I felt like being particularly cautious that evening, I walked the rest of the way. There were a lot of strollers already on the streets, and I was glad to mingle with them and lose myself. I saw a large knot of young people enjoying the spring night around the Belleville Metro station. Then I walked under the crumbling archway that had once closed off the Cité de Trévise and found myself in the small square that Skopje had mentioned. It had the look of old Paris—a tiny park with a fountain.

There were three hotels on the square, all small, and Duke's Bar was situated in one of them. I went in and looked around. The place was deserted—obviously the way Skopje had wanted it. I found him sitting at a table near a rear door that led to a back room. I walked over to him.

"Flowers are blooming at the Tuileries," I said.

He studied my face. He was a tall, lanky man with a sallow face and dark rings under his eyes. "It will be an early spring," he said carefully.

I sat down across the table from him. We were alone in the place, except for the waiter at the bar. "I'm Nick Carter," I said. "And you're Jan Skopje."

"Yes. It is a pleasure to meet you, Mr. Carter." His manner was even more nervous than his voice had been on the phone. "We must make this meeting brief. I believe they have found out where I am living. I don't know what they have in mind, but I don't want them to see me with you."

"Bulgarian agents?" I asked.

"I am not sure. They might be Topcon men. They—"

A waiter came and took our order. Skopje waited until he had brought the drinks and left again before he resumed the discussion.

"There is a man watching my hotel," he said quietly. He looked over his shoulder toward the swinging doors of the back room where the waiter had just disappeared. Then he turned back to me. "The stolen device will be taken aboard the Orient Express two days from now at Lausanne, Switzerland. The train stops there in early morning."

"Why Lausanne?" I asked.

"Topcon headquarters is in Switzerland. I don't know where." He watched the front entrance of the place closely. The waiter came back into the room and went to the bar.

"Who will be carrying the stolen device?" I asked.

"This is a particularly big operation for Topcon. Therefore, the head of the organization will convey the stolen property."

"And who is that?"

Skopje opened his mouth to speak, but no words came out. His eyes opened wide, and his mouth dropped open even farther. I heard a faint noise behind the swinging doors at Skopje's back and saw one of them moving. Skopje's jaw was working soundlessly as he grabbed in vain at a place in the middle of his back. Then he slumped forward on the table.

I reached for Wilhelmina as I rose from my chair. Then I saw the small dart sticking out of Skopje's back. "Skopje?" I said, lifting his head. But he was already dead.

Just then the waiter turned toward us and saw what had happened. I ignored his shouts and slammed through the swinging doors to a small kitchen and storage area. A door leading to the alley was open.

Moving through the dark doorway, I entered the alley cautiously, Luger in hand. There were heavy shadows, and at first I saw nothing. Then I caught a glimpse of a dark figure emerging in the lighter street beyond.

I ran down the alley, and as I reached the sidewalk, stopped and looked to my right. The man was running down the block, people staring after him.

I holstered the big Luger and started after him. He rounded a corner, and I followed. I was gaining on him. He rounded another corner, and we were on the Rue Bergère. Dazzling neon lights splashed against the darkness. The man was still running up ahead. I kept after him. Tourists and native Parisians stopped and stared. The man disappeared down a narrow side street, and I lost him again.

I ran to the entrance of the street and looked down it into the blackness. He was nowhere in sight. I saw only doorways and a couple of alleys and another intersecting side street. I pulled Wilhelmina out again and proceeded more cautiously. He could be anywhere, and I had the disadvantage of having to flush him out.

I checked each doorway as I passed. They were all empty. It was just possible that he had made it all the way to the intersecting street before I had reached the corner. I passed an alleyway and saw nothing in it. I moved slowly to the next one, sure now that I had lost him.

As I stepped into the entrance of the alley, there was a movement beside me. Something came down hard on my right wrist, and I lost Wilhelmina. Big hands were grabbing me and hurling me off my feet, and I thudded to the cobblestones, bruising my back and shoulder.

When I looked up, I saw that there were two figures standing over me. One was the thin, mustachioed man whom I had been chasing along the Paris streets and beside him was his big, bald hulking comrade, the man who had clobbered me with a piece of board and knocked me to the ground. The thin one held a length of iron pipe, a foot and a half long, in his hand. I wondered if they had lured me here to kill me.

"Who are you?" I asked, hoping to stall them. "Why did you kill Skopje?"

"*Ça ne vous regarde pas,*" the big man said, telling me it was none of my business.

"*Dépechez-vous,*" the other one added, urging the big man to get on with it.

He did. He kicked out at my face with a hob-nailed shoe. I grabbed at the foot and stopped it from crushing my head in. I twisted hard, rolling so I could keep the pressure on. In a moment there was a crack of bone as his ankle broke. He yelled and hit the pavement.

The wiry one swung the pipe at me, and as I rolled away, it cracked loudly on the paving stones near me. The pipe descended again, but this time I grabbed it and pulled hard. He fell to the ground on top of me, losing the pipe. He then struggled to free himself, but while he was flailing about, I chopped at his neck and heard the snap of bone. He was dead when he hit the pavement.

When I got to my feet, the big man was trying to get back into the act. Just as he struggled to one knee, I kicked him solidly in the head, and he crashed to the pavement. Dead.

I looked for and found Wilhelmina, then went through their pockets. There was no I.D. Because they had spoken French, I figured it was more likely that these were Topcon men from Switzerland rather than Bulgarian agents. Jan Skopje had confided to AXE that he had worked for KGB and Topcon and had helped plan the theft of the monitor device. When Skopje had defected, either Topcon or KGB had to shut him up. It had evidently been Topcon's job.

I had just about given up on finding anything of value on the bodies when I discovered a small slip of crumpled paper in a pocket of the slim man. It was in French: *Klaus Pfaff. A Gasthaus Lucerne, L. Minuit le deuze.*

I noticed a tag on the inside of his jacket; it bore the initials *H.D.* As I slipped the paper into my pocket, I examined the slim man's physical appearance carefully. Then I hurried into the shadows of the Parisian night.

Three

Early the next morning I checked out some small hotels in the Cité de Trévise, and on the third stop I ran into a little luck. Two men had registered the day before yesterday. One had been slim and the other had been a big man. The slim man had signed in as Henri Depeu, a name that matched the initials in the man's jacket. The big one had been called Navarro.

I could make some guesses by putting my scraps of information together. Depeu was to report to a man called Klaus Pfaff after he had disposed of Skopje and me. The *L* after *gasthaus* on the note probably meant Lausanne. At least that was what I had to presume. Depeu was to meet Pfaff at the time designated, midnight, and tell him how things had gone here in Paris. Presumably, Pfaff would then report to the head of Topcon. Unless Pfaff himself were the big man.

My course of action was clear to me. I would go to Lausanne because that was where the stolen monitor would go aboard the Orient Express. And I would meet Pfaff in Depeu's place. If Pfaff himself was not the Topcon chief who would carry the device on the train, he probably would know the identity of the leader. Maybe I could persuade him to reveal that secret identity.

I could have caught the Orient Express in Paris at the Gare de Lyon, but since I expected to spend quite some time aboard later and since time was of the essence, I hired a car to drive to Lausanne. I rented a Mercedes-Benz 280SL, a sporty yellow one that still had the new smell inside. By late morning I was out of Paris and on the road to Troyes and Dijon. The weather had warmed up, and the driving was pleasant. The countryside was rolling and green, but it became more hilly as I got closer to Switzerland.

In mid-afternoon I crossed into Switzerland, and the road became narrow and winding for a while. Snowy peaks were appearing in the distance, but they stayed in the background for the rest of the drive. Just outside Lausanne, in the grassy hills of the surrounding countryside, I spotted a car that had broken down on the shoulder of the road. A girl was looking under its hood. I pulled over and stopped, offering to help.

"Anything I can do?" I asked as I walked over to the bright blue Lotus Plus 2.

She looked up and studied me carefully. She was a beautiful, long-limbed blonde in a leather miniskirt and boots. Her hair was not quite shoulder length and had a windblown look about it. After she had focused on me for a moment, her face lit up.

"Nick!" she said. "Nick Carter!"

Now it was my turn to take a second look. "I'm afraid you have the advantage," I said uncertainly. "I don't believe—"

"Bonn, last year about this time," she said in her German accent. "The Gröning case. Nick, you don't remember!"

Then I remembered, too. "Ursula?"

She smiled a wide, sexy smile.

"Ursula Bergman," I added.

"Yes," she answered, the smile radiating from her lovely face. "How nice of you to come along, just to aid an old friend in distress."

"You had brown hair in Bonn," I said. "Short, brown hair. And brown eyes."

"This is my real hair," she said, touching the flaxen-colored strands. "And the eyes were contact lenses."

Ursula laughed a melodic laugh. We had worked together for about a week in Bonn and Hamburg last year to gather information on a left-wing German named Karl Gröning who was suspected of passing West German military information to certain persons in East Berlin. Ursula had been on special assignment in that case. Her regular work was with a division of West German intelligence that concerned itself solely with the tracking down and apprehension of ex-Nazis who had committed war crimes. That was all AXE had told me about her, and I had had little opportunity to learn more.

"I didn't keep up with the Gröning case after I was called back to Washington," I said. "Did the courts in Bonn find him guilty as charged?"

She nodded smugly. "He is presently whiling away his time in a German prison."

"Good. You like to hear some happy endings to these cases occasionally. What are you doing in Switzerland, Ursula, or shouldn't I ask?"

She shrugged her lovely shoulders. "The same old thing."

"I see."

"And what are you doing in Switzerland?"

I grinned. "The same old thing."

We both laughed. It was pleasant seeing each other again. "What's wrong with the Lotus?"

"I'm afraid the fan belt is *kaput*, Nick. Do you think I can beg a ride into town?"

"It would be my pleasure," I answered.

We got into the Mercedes, and I backed out onto the road and headed for town. After I had gotten into high gear, I looked over at her as she continued talking about Karl Gröning, and I saw how her breasts pushed against the jersey blouse and how the miniskirt hiked up high on her long full thighs. Ursula had blossomed since I knew her in Bonn, and the result was impressive.

"Are you stopping in Lausanne?" Ursula asked as I shifted onto a winding downgrade. The panorama of Lausanne was appearing before us, the town nestled in the hills with patches of snow from the recent winter's snowfalls above it.

"Just tonight," I said. "Maybe we could get together for a drink in some discreet little rathskeller."

"Oh, I would enjoy that very much. But I'm busy this evening, and I must leave tomorrow morning."

"Do you think your car will be ready by then?"

"I go by train in the morning," she said.

There was only one train leaving Lausanne the next morning, and that was the Orient Express, my train. "How interesting," I commented. "I leave by train tomorrow morning, too."

She looked over at me with her clear blue eyes. We were both assessing the significance of this coincidence. If we had not worked together, if we were not familiar with each other's employers, both of us would have been suspicious. But I had seen Ursula Bergman at work, and I trusted my judgment that she was no double agent.

She had already made her decision. Her eyes flashed genuine friendliness. "Why, that's very nice, Nick. We'll be able to have a drink together on board."

"I'll look forward to it." I smiled.

When we got into town, I dropped Ursula off at the Hotel de la Paix on the Avenue B. Constant, in the heart of town, and then I drove to an

innocuous little pension in the Place St.
François.

When I got to my room, I opened up my luggage and started to get ready for my meeting. I
was going to make myself up to look like Henri
Depeu, and I had to do it from memory.

I got out the case that the Special Effects and
Editing boys had given me. It was a disguise kit,
an imaginative one at that. Hawk himself had
put a lot of it together—he had been a disguise
expert in his day. The kit included strips of plastic "skin" and various colored contact lenses,
wigs and toupees, and a lot of different shades of
make-up. There were even plastic scars that
could be affixed to any portion of the face or
body.

I set the kit up in front of the dressing-table
mirror. I applied the plastic "skin" first, building
up layers to thicken the bridge of my nose and
lengthen the tip. Then I built up my cheekbones
to make my cheeks look sunken below the
build-up. After I lengthened my earlobes and
chin, my face began to resemble Depeu's. Then I
put on make-up that matched his coloring, insert-
ed brown contact lenses, and chose a light brown
wig. I looked at myself in the mirror. I wouldn't
really pass for Depeu if anyone looked too closely,
but I might fool Pfaff momentarily.

At eleven-thirty I drove across the Pont
Bessères on Rue de la Caroline to the Gasthaus

Lucerne. When I entered, I was sorry to see that there were a half dozen customers in the place.

I had no way of knowing what Klaus Pfaff looked like. I could only hope that I had beaten him there and that when he arrived, he would recognize my pseudo-Depeu face.

Twelve o'clock came, the time of the appointment, and nothing happened. A young student couple had come in and taken a table at the front, I had asked for one near the back of the room, facing the door. Five after came, and then ten after. I was beginning to think that Pfaff was not going to show or that he was already there. There was only one man alone, and he was a barrel-bellied German type. I did not think he could be Pfaff. A whole new group of customers came in, and the place was humming. I did not have the slightest idea how I would handle Pfaff under these circumstances. Quarter after twelve arrived, and I was forced to order a sandwich and beer. Just after the waiter had brought my order, the door opened, and a short, thin man entered. There appeared to be a bulge under his suit jacket. He stopped just inside the door and looked around. When his eyes found me, he started right for my table. This had to be Klaus Pfaff.

He stopped at my table and looked around the room again before seating himself. He was a nervous man, with slicked-down blondish hair and a thin scar across his left ear. "*Bonjour,* Klaus," I said to him.

He seated himself across from me. "Sorry to be late," he said. "And please speak English. You know the rules."

He had not really looked squarely at me yet, and I was grateful. The waiter returned and took an order of knockwurst and sauerkraut from Pfaff. While that was going on, I eased Wilhelmina out of my jacket pocket and trained the Luger on Pfaff. Nobody had seen the gun yet.

The waiter was gone. Pfaff glanced at me and then peered over his shoulder. "All right. What happened in Paris?"

The idea had occurred to me when I was preparing for this meeting that Pfaff might just be the head of Topcon, the one who was to carry the stolen goods. But now that I saw him before me, I knew that he could not be the leader.

"Quite a lot happened in Paris," I said.

My voice startled him. He focused on my face for the first time, and his eyes narrowed. I saw them size me up. Then his face changed as he gazed at my face again.

"No, I am not Henri Depeu," I said.

Anger and fear showed plainly on his narrow face. "What is this?" he asked in a low voice.

"Where I come from, we call it truth or consequences."

"Who are you? Where is Henri?"

"Henri is dead," I said. "And I killed him."

His eyes slitted down even further and his mouth twitched slightly at the corner. "I don't know whether you are telling the truth or not. I am leaving. My meeting was with Depeu."

He started to rise, but I stopped him.

"I wouldn't do that," I warned.

He hesitated, still in his chair. His eyes flicked to my right arm, which held the Luger under the table.

"Yes," I said quietly. "I am holding a gun on you. And I intend to use it if you get up from that chair."

Pfaff swallowed and studied my face. I could see his mind working, trying to figure out who I was and trying to assess my purpose. "You would not dare shoot a gun in here," he said.

"I can be through the back entrance within fifteen seconds of your hitting the floor." I hoped he would accept the bluff. "And I have friends waiting outside. Do you want to try me?"

The anger in his face was gone now; fear had taken control of it. He was not a brave man—which was good for me.

"What do you want?" he asked.

"Information."

He laughed nervously. "The Tourist Bureau is down the street."

I sighed. "Be coy with me, and I'll blow your head off."

His grin faded. "What kind of information do you want?"

"I think we'd better discuss it in private," I

said. I reached into my jacket pocket with my free hand and threw a wad of Swiss francs to pay for our orders on the table. "The meal is on me," I said with a small smile. "Now, I want you to get up and walk very slowly to the front entrance. I'll be right behind you, and this gun will be aimed at your back. When we get on the street, I'll give you further instructions."

"Do you think you can get away with this stupid thing?" he demanded.

"You'd better hope I do."

I stuck Wilhelmina into my pocket, and we went outside. I walked him to the Mercedes and told him to get into the driver's seat. I got in beside him, flipped him the keys, and told him to start driving toward the edge of town.

Pfaff was getting very frightened now. But he drove the car into the green hills as I had ordered. I directed him onto a dirt road that ran off to the right into some trees and ordered him to stop when we were out of sight of the main road. When the motor was off, I turned and leveled the Luger at his head.

"You are committing suicide with this farce," he said loudly.

"Because your Topcon hoods will get me?"

His lips worked together. That was the first time I had mentioned the organization. "That is correct," he said flatly.

"We'll see, but in the meantime, you're going to cooperate with me, aren't you?"

"What do you want to know?"

"I want to know who is boarding the Orient Express tomorrow morning."

"Many people."

"I know already that Topcon's chief is going to carry the stolen device on the train personally," I said. "But you can tell me who he is, and give me a description of him."

"You must be insane." He looked incredulous.

I was not in the mood for insults. I swung the Luger down across the side of his face. He grunted and fell away from the blow as blood ran down his cheek. His breath became shallow as he grabbed at the wound.

"I don't want any more talk like that," I growled at him. "I want answers to the questions I ask you. And you'd better start talking fast."

"All right," he finally agreed. "May I smoke a cigarette?"

I hesitated. "Go ahead." I watched closely as he took one out and lighted it. He opened the ashtray on the dash and put the match in it.

"Will you guarantee my safety if I cooperate with you?" he asked, his hand still at the ahstray.

"That's right."

"Then I'll give you the name you want. It is—"

But Pfaff had no intention of telling me anything. His hand had released the catch on the ashtray and pulled it free of the dashboard. He flung the load of ashes into my face.

While my eyes were full of ashes, he hit my right arm and knocked it violently aside. He had a lot of strength for a small man. Then the car door was open, and Pfaff was out and running.

I swore aloud as I cleared my burning eyes. I still held the Luger. I stumbled out of the car. By now my eyes were clear enough to see Pfaff running headlong toward the main road.

"Stop!" I yelled, but he kept moving. I aimed a shot at his legs. The Luger roared, and the bullet kicked up at Pfaff's feet. I had missed.

Pfaff turned and ducked into the trees to the left of the dirt road. I ran after him.

I had removed Pfaff's shoulder gun when he had gotten into the Mercedes, so I figured I had an advantage, but I was wrong. As I moved into a small clearing, a shot rang out from Pfaff's direction and whistled past my ear. He must have had a small gun hidden on him somewhere.

As I ducked behind a thick pine tree, I heard Pfaff moving just a few feet ahead. I started out more cautiously. I slipped the Luger into its holster, for we were very near the main road, and I did not want to add my gunfire to the noise. Besides, I wanted Pfaff alive.

After another twenty yards, just when I thought I might have lost him, Pfaff broke cover not far from me and started running off across a clearing. I decided to be less cautious. I sprinted after him, hoping he wouldn't hear me until it was too late. As I got to within twenty feet of him, he turned and saw me. He had just raised the small automatic to aim when I hit him in a diving tackle around the waist.

The gun went off twice, missing me both times as we plummeted to the ground. We rolled around a couple of times. Then I got hold of his gun hand, and we both struggled to our feet. I rammed a fist into Pfaff's face and twisted at the gun arm. The automatic fell from his grasp.

But Pfaff was not finished. He raised his knee savagely into my groin. While I was recovering from the blow, he broke loose, turned, and ran again.

I fought the pain in my gut and started after him. We slashed through underbrush and tree branches. I gained on him every second. Then I was hurtling myself at him again. We both went down, my hands grabbing at him and his fists pummeling my face and head. We crashed into a dead tree, which crumbled under our impact. I had a good hold on the man now, but he was still flailing with his hands. Then I smashed a fist into his face, and he fell back to the ground.

"Now, damn you, tell me the name," I demanded breathlessly.

Pfaff reached into a pocket. I wondered what weapon he would come up with this time. I moved my forearm and let the stiletto drop into my palm as Pfaff's hand came out of his pocket and went to his mouth.

It took me a split-second to realize what was

happening. Pfaff, knowing he was a goner, had popped a cyanide capsule into his mouth. He was biting down on it.

I threw the stiletto to the ground and dropped to my knees beside him. I grabbed at his jaw and tried to pry it open, but my attempt was unsuccessful.

Then it was over. Pfaff's eyes widened, and I felt his body go rigid in my grasp. I let go of his jaw, and it fell open. There was an unpleasant odor. Then I saw the tiny rivulet of blood at the corner of his mouth and the broken glass on his tongue. Slowly, his face was turning a darker color.

Klaus Pfaff was dead.

Four

The diesel engine of the Orient Express slid almost silently into the Lausanne station as the sun was just coming up beyond a distant hill. There were few people waiting on the platform. I watched as the train rumbled to a stop and read the lettering on the side of the cars: PARIS LAUSANNE MILANO TRIESTE BELGRADE SOFIA ISTANBUL. They were exotic names, and they revived memories of many of my past assignments.

The train had stopped, and a few passengers were disembarking. By now a larger crowd had gathered on the platform to board. I scanned the faces casually. One of them might be the man with the monitor, unless Klaus Pfaff's disappearance had made Topcon think twice about moving the device on this train. But I did not think so. Apparently, plans had already been made to meet and do business with the KGB on this train. Those plans could not be changed so easily.

After another look at the faces around me, I picked up my luggage and started to board the train. Then I heard the voice behind me.

44

"Good morning, Nick."

I turned and saw Ursula Bergman. *"Guten morgen,* Ursula," I said.

"Did you enjoy your evening in Lausanne?"

"It was pleasantly quiet," I lied. I noticed that despite the smile, Ursula had a new look on her face today. There was a tension there that had not been noticeable before. "Say, I hear we have a dining car until Milan. Can I buy you breakfast aboard?"

She hesitated only a moment, and then gave me a big smile. "I would like that."

While I was boarding, I tried to get a look at most of the passengers who got on, but it was very difficult. A half hour later we slid quietly into the Swiss countryside, and soon we were running along at a good speed through the green hills. Ursula and I met in the dining car at eight-thirty and had no trouble getting a table.

"The Swiss scenery is fantastic, isn't it?" I was making small talk.

Ursula seemed preoccupied. "Oh yes," she responded with false enthusiasm.

"It looks a great deal like Bavaria here," I continued.

She had not heard me for a moment. "Oh. There is a similarity. I see it now."

I smiled gently at her. "Ursula, something is wrong, isn't it?"

She looked quickly at me with serious blue eyes. "I don't know if I want to get you involved in my problems, Nick. After all, you have your own case to worry about."

I placed my hand on hers. "Listen, if you're in trouble, maybe I can help somehow. My soul belongs to AXE, but they can spare a half hour or so of my time."

She looked up and smiled at the small joke. "I was supposed to meet a man last night. Another agent with our organization. He was to board the train at Lausanne with me, and we were to—carry out an assignment together."

"And he didn't board?"

Her voice became tight with anger. "He—I found him in his hotel room—"

So that was it. Ursula and her fellow agent were apparently after another of their many ex-Nazis, and the companion had gotten too close to their prey and become the victim himself. "Was it one of your Third Reich friends?" I asked.

She glanced up, and her eyes told me yes. "I am not frightened, Nick. My fellow agent was assigned to the case just to back me up. Unfortunately, he must have been recognized. I don't think they know who I am yet."

"I don't want to pry into things you shouldn't be telling me. But we can relax the rules a little bit, I think. You're after a war criminal and you expect him to be aboard this train. Am I right?"

"An informant told us he would be here."

"Can you get other help if you need it?"

"No chance. Not on such short notice. But I have been telling myself that perhaps I could count on you for some assistance should the situation arise."

"You can count on it," I assured her.

Ursula nodded. She was a tough cookie. She'd had much experience with the "wet affairs"—as the Russians so nicely described them—that went with intelligence work.

A waiter brought out toast and coffee and left. I glanced down the aisle and saw an Oriental, apparently a Chinese, seated alone. He looked back at me and then quickly turned his attention to his breakfast.

Wondering if the Chinese could be a professional, I searched my memory for a name that might match his pudgy face. My boss Hawk was very insistent on certain precautions that he called the fundamentals of our trade, one of them being a requirement that agents of my rank periodically study files on the other side's active operatives. Consequently I carried quite a memory bank around with me.

In this case, I failed to come up with a name. I couldn't identify the Chinese. That didn't rule him out as an adversary. He could be a recent recruit to the intelligence ranks, someone who had become active since I last did my homework. For all I knew, he might even be connected with Topcon.

Another man, an Occidental, came in and

joined the Chinese. I watched them with interest, wondering what they were talking about. Curiosity might have killed the cat, but it never harmed anyone in my business. It was a lack of curiosity that sometimes proved fatal.

I took a sip of coffee and watched a new couple enter the dining car. They came down the aisle and took a table near the one where I sat with Ursula. The woman was about thirty, with dark brown hair and a good figure. The man was of medium height with brown hair and a strong chin under a prominent nose.

"What is it, Nick?" asked Ursula.

I shook my head. "Nothing." My memory bank had just produced something on the man with the prominent nose. His name was Ivan Lubyanka and he was a KGB agent.

For the moment, I pushed the Chinese and his companion out of my mind. The appearance of Lubyanka meant something. He was high in the KGB ranks, the type of man the Russians would send to negotiate an important deal with an organization like Topcon.

Lubyanka and the woman with him appeared to be going through the formal amenities exchanged by strangers. His behavior, and hers, indicated they had just met.

I was carrying a small limpet microphone in my pocket. I wished I had it stuck to the table where Lubyanka and the woman sat, and that I was back in my compartment listening to their conversation. I was sure it would be extremely interesting.

"Do you know that man, Nick?" Ursula asked me.

"He looks a little familiar." I put her off. She had enough to worry about.

"Maybe it's the woman who interests you," she suggested, showing me the trace of a smile.

"Hardly," I assured her. "She can't hold a candle to you."

That, at least, was true. One of my pleasant memories of my past acquaintance with Ursula included a brief interlude in the bedroom.

Apparently the same thought had occurred to the German girl. She laughed softly and reached across the table and touched my hand. "Too bad this is a business trip, Nick."

"Maybe it won't be all business. I may get your clothes off yet," I said.

While we talked, I was still watching Lubyanka and the woman. Their conversation appeared to be growing more intense. I had already decided that Lubyanka was the Russian agent assigned to buy the monitoring device from Topcon. But what about the woman? I didn't think Lubyanka had picked her up on the train for fun and games. AXE's report on him said he was strictly business, with no discernible weaknesses except possibly the belief that communism was the wave of the future. I would have bet my trusty Wilhelmina that the lady was also a spy.

As I gave that some thought, the woman happened to glance in my direction. Her eyes were cool and shrewd, and her gaze was very direct. Then she pulled her attention back to the KGB man and they plunged into discussion again.

I weighed the possibility that the woman was Topcon's representative, that she had the monitoring device I was assigned to recover. But I had been told that Topcon's boss was bringing the device aboard the train in order to handle the bargaining. Could it be that this woman was the brains behind a super-tough organization like Topcon?

If that happened to be the case, I thought, she might be an intriguing lady to meet.

"Nick, I've decided to tell you about the man I'm after. I can't ask your help if I don't level with you," Ursula broke in on my thoughts. "We have been looking for him for twenty-five years. He was a killer of the worst kind. When he was in charge of a prison camp in Poland, those who died quickly at his hands were considered lucky."

The German girl turned and stared out of the big window beside us. A chalet-dotted countryside slipped past. The click of the rails beneath the train was a rhythmic undercurrent to her low voice.

"It was in Belgrade that we picked up his

trail. Those of us who have seen reports on his career call him the Butcher—the Butcher of Belgrade. He is both dangerous and cunning. Although we have come close to capturing him more than once, he has continued to elude us. He changes names and identities and even his face. We know nothing about his present life and we don't know exactly what he looks like now. We do know that people who were acquainted with him in the past spotted him recently in Belgrade. And he is supposed to be traveling on this train with us."

"I can see that this is more than just another assignment. Capturing him is very important to you."

"Yes, it is. The things he did ..." She didn't finish the sentence. She didn't need to finish it.

I swallowed the last of my coffee. "We'll keep in touch, Ursula. It isn't a very big train. I'll be around if you need me. You are armed, aren't you?"

"Yes."

"Good." I glanced across the aisle and saw that Lubyanka and the woman were leaving together.

"Excuse me," I said, taking some bills out of my pocket and placing them on the table. I rose from my seat. "We'll get together later."

Lubyanka and the brown-haired woman were leaving the dining car. They were headed toward the end of the train, rather than back toward the

Class A compartments. I followed them out of the car, taking a quick look at the Chinese as I passed. His face was not familiar, but he glanced at me again as I walked by.

There was a small observation platform on the rear of the train, and the mysterious woman and Lubyanka went directly to it. They stood there and continued their conversation. They did not see me as I stood in the smoking salon behind them. I reached into my jacket pocket and pulled out a small disc-like limpet microphone. With that gadget I might just be able to find out what they were saying. I went on the platform with them.

The sound of my approach was drowned out by the movement of the train, but so were their voices. I made an obvious sound, and they turned. The woman gave me a hostile look; Lubyanka studied me carefully. He did not appear to recognize me.

"Good morning," I said with a French accent. "It is a lovely morning, is it not?"

The woman turned away from me impatiently. Lubyanka grunted out, "Yes, a beautiful morning."

"How far are you going?" I asked. I pretended I was losing my balance, and grabbed at the rail near Lubyanka, depositing the limpet on the underside of the rail.

Now Lubyanka's face was also hostile. "It all depends," he said. He did not want to be bothered by an intruder any more than the woman did. He turned coldly away from me and stared out over the receding tracks that glinted brightly in the morning sun.

"Well, have a good day," I said to them.

Lubyanka nodded without looking at me. I turned and went back inside. When I passed through the dining car, Ursula had gone. I went to the sleeping car and entered my compartment, number three. Then I opened up my luggage and located the small receiver set that was hidden in it. I snapped it on and turned a dial.

At first all I got was static. Then I heard the steady click-click of the wheels of the train and the voices interspersed with it.

"It is necessary ... see the device ... make an offer." It was Lubyanka's voice.

More static, then the woman's voice.

"... not reveal the device ... if we allowed you to examine . . . but there are good photographs ... to my compartment later."

Lubyanka's voice then uttered a curt farewell to the woman, and the conversation was over.

I snapped the receiver off and hid it in my luggage. There was no doubt in my mind now. The woman was the Topcon agent, and she was dealing with Lubyanka for sale of the stolen monitor device.

The question still remained, though, whether the woman was on the train alone or whether she was traveling with another Topcon operative, possibly the head of the organization, who was keeping out of sight per Jan Skopje's prediction. If she was on board alone, it was possible that she was the head of Topcon. In any case, she would probably not be carrying the device on her person, and it might not even be in her compartment. I had to check to make sure.

A light lunch was served in the diner just before we hit Milan. I met Ursula, and we ate together. I thought of the pleasure she could afford in one of the sleeping compartments. But I did not have time to think about sex for long. I had to find out which compartment the Topcon woman occupied.

I was able to accomplish my mission when the train stopped at Milan and the dining car was taken off. Ursula had stepped off the train briefly, to get a look at the passengers who had gotten off to stretch their legs, and I had gone with her. Just as the train was about to leave, I saw the Topcon woman emerge from a station doorway and get aboard the second of two sleeper cars, the one next to Voiture 7, where I was staying. I left Ursula on the platform and quickly moved into Voiture 5. As I entered the corridor, I saw the woman disappearing into a compartment. I moved down the corridor and noted that she had entered Compartment 4. I continued to the end of the car and stepped out onto the platform. A tall dark-haired man in his fifties—but with a youthful, virile look—climbed aboard the car; he was carrying a portable radio, an excellent German brand, but it was silent. He passed me with a curt nod, and went on into the sleeper. I remembered that I had seen him at the Lausanne station. After he had passed, I got off the train again and found Ursula.

She had been watching faces, but she had not found her man yet. She was becoming angry.

"Do you know how long he will be aboard?" I asked as we climbed back aboard together.

He may be getting off at Belgrade, but I'm not sure. He may have gotten wind that we are tracking him and not boarded at all."

We watched the uniformed train official on the platform swing his "poached egg," the disc on a stick that signaled the train's departure from the station. There was a small jerking movement and then the train was moving on. Many people were waving from the platform.

I was standing very close to Ursula. I put my hand on her waist. "Do you think you'll know your man if you see him?"

She glanced at me and then out at the station as it slid past us and fell behind the train. "As an SS man in the Third Reich, he was a blond. He has probably dyed his hair. He wore a mustache then, but he may have shaved it off. Still, there are things I can look for. He is a man about your size. He used to have a bullet scar on his neck. I realize that could have been surgically removed, but I can still look for it."

"That isn't much to go on."

"There's something else. He has a malformed knuckle on his left hand. That would be difficult to change."

"It still isn't much. But I'll watch for a man who keeps his left hand in his pocket all the time," I said jokingly.

Ursula gave me a small smile. "If I see someone who might be him, Nick, I have hope of tricking him into giving his identity away."

She sounded determined. But her devotion to duty was not the only thing about her that I found appealing.

I slid my arm around her and she turned suddenly, her lips slightly parted. I pressed my mouth to hers, and she responded.

After a moment, she pulled away. "I see you still enjoy keeping your fellow agents in a happy frame of mind," she said.

I noticed the way her breasts pressed against the sweater she was wearing. "You know me, I like to keep everyone smiling," I said.

She was a little flustered, maybe a little embarrassed, by the way she had responded to the kiss. "I must go to my compartment now, Nick. I'll—see you later."

I smiled easily. "I'm counting on it." Then she was gone.

We were out in open country again. It was a sunny spring afternoon. The Italian countryside was splashed with the vivid colors of crimson poppies and blue wildflowers. Venice was our next stop in late afternoon, and I expected to find out about the Topcon woman before we arrived there.

I walked through the daycoaches that contained both first and second class sitting compartments. The second class part was much noisier and less civilized than the first class part. The first class compartments had closeable doors, and many of them had curtains drawn for privacy. I moved from one car to the next slowly, watching the faces of the travelers as they chatted or played cards or just sat and dozed, letting the movement of the train draw them into slumber. On the last car before the sleepers, I saw the brown-haired woman again. She was sitting with two men; neither of them was Lubyanka. One of the men was the one with the radio who had passed me getting back on board at Milan. She sat and knitted, glancing out the window, and did not appear to know either man. The man with the radio was immersed in an Italian newspaper. The other man, a fat, bald fellow, was munching happily on a lunch he had brought aboard with him and was seemingly oblivious of the other two. I walked past the compartment before the woman could see me, and headed for Voiture 5. This was my chance to take a look in her compartment.

I was alone in the corridor when I arrived at her door. I knocked once to be sure no comrade of hers, or a porter, was inside. Then I picked the lock quickly and entered, closing the door behind me.

It was a typical sleeping compartment, with a single bunk on one side of the small room and a nightstand and mirror on the other wall. There were racks for luggage, just as in the day coaches, and the woman had several suitcases.

I took down one piece of luggage at a time and went through all of them. I found nothing, not even the photographs that she had mentioned in her talk with Lubyanka. I did find an immigration paper that identified her as Eva Schmidt, a Swiss national.

I was disappointed in the luggage. I began a systematic search of the compartment, looking through bedding and everything else that might conceal the device. I was almost finished when the door burst open. One of the two men who stood there was the Chinese I had seen earlier in the dining car. With him was his dining companion, an Occidental with a swarthy, pockmarked face.

Each of the intruders carried a revolver. And each of the weapons was pointed at me.

I smiled at them. "Gentlemen, you should have knocked."

The swarthy man kicked the door shut. "Do you want me to kill him now?" he asked the Chinese.

There was very little to stop them. Their guns

carried silencers. If they put a few bullets in me, no one outside the compartment would know.

"Don't be impatient," the Chinese told the swarthy man in excellent English.

Although the Oriental's face was pudgy and his thick neck rippled with rolls of fat, his shoulders looked powerful and his hands were immense. I didn't doubt that he had the ability to take care of himself in a fight.

The swarthy man was short and heavy and his belly lapped over his belt. He looked as though he spent too much of his spare time boozing. The eyes in his pockmarked face were set close together. I rated him behind the Chinese as an adversary, as slower and possibly less intelligent than his companion.

"Did you find what you were looking for?" the Chinese asked me.

I shrugged. "What do you think I was looking for?"

"That sort of response is very stupid, Mr. Carter. If you are going to pretend you don't know what I'm talking about, I might as well let my friend here go ahead and shoot you."

"I certainly wouldn't want that to happen." I spread my hands out, palms up. "I'm empty handed, as you can see."

"Perhaps Eva Schmidt is not carrying the device," said the swarthy man.

"That is, of course, a possibility. How do you feel about it, Mr. Carter?" the Chinese asked.

"I wouldn't know. I haven't had a chance to get acquainted with Miss Schmidt. How is it that you know my name?"

"It's in our files, along with your photograph. You are close to being a celebrity in our field, you know. I had hoped we might be running into each other."

"Your files must be more complete than ours. I tried to place you when I saw you in the dining car. I couldn't."

The Chinese chuckled. "There aren't any photographs of me in western files, Mr. Carter."

That gave me something to think about. It put him in a very special category.

The Chinese sat down on the edge of Eva Schmidt's bunk. "Enough about me, Mr. Carter. I am a modest man. I'd rather not discuss myself. I prefer to have you tell us how much you know about the organization that calls itself Topcon."

I saw no reason for keeping that a secret. "Very little," I said. "I don't even know if Eva Schmidt is the organization's boss or only one of the hired hands."

"As a matter of fact, she is neither," the Chinese remarked. He appeared amused that he had more information on Topcon than I had. "The Schmidt woman is not the boss and yet she is certainly more than a mere underling."

The swarthy man, who was leaning against the door, stirred restlessly. "You're telling him more than he's telling us," he grumbled to the Chinese.

"Since we intend to kill him, that hardly matters," replied the Chinese in his deceptively amiable voice.

I shifted my feet slightly so that I was in a position to move toward either man. I didn't plan to be shot down without trying to take them first. When I made my move, I would go for the one who was closest.

"You aren't even supposed to be here. Topcon is selling the device to the Russians," I told the Chinese.

"They also offered it to us. We weren't willing to pay their price. We decided to take it instead."

I leaned forward slightly, letting my weight go with the movement so that I was prepared to spring toward the man on the bed. "You mean this train may be swarming with all kinds of agents who hope to steal the device from the people who stole it in the first place?"

"That's the trouble with what you capitalists call free enterprise. It arouses the spirit of competition," the Chinese said with a chuckle.

The swarthy man spoke again. "We'd better get on with this. The woman could come back at any time."

"And we will get on with it, my friend. But it isn't every day that one has an opportunity to talk firsthand to an American Killmaster. How many of my comrades have you disposed of in your infamous career, Mr. Carter?"

I shrugged. "I'm a modest man too."

"You have been quite a thorn in our side. When I report that I have gained possession of the monitor and have eliminated you as well, I may be commended by the Chairman himself," said the Chinese in a gloating voice.

They were a lovely pair, I thought. The swarthy man wanted to kill me instantly out of sheer impatience and the Chinese was interested in the glory he could win by returning to Peking with my scalp on his belt.

With his left hand, the Chinese gestured to his companion. Then he raised the revolver in his right. He was ready to execute me and he wasn't going to take any chances. He planned for both of them to pump slugs into my body.

"I lied to you," I said.

The Chinese hesitated, his finger on the trigger. The man at the door cursed. "He's stalling, Sheng Tze."

Sheng Tze, I thought, and suddenly the memory bank was working. Sheng Tze, the legendary Chinese Communist agent who had been so successful at shielding his identity that he was more like a ghost than flesh and blood. At various times I had heard him described as an old man; at others, I had heard people insist that, no, he was only in his thirties. And none of those people had known him well. They had only caught fleeting glimpses of him, apparently in a variety of disguises. For the secret of Sheng Tze's remaining a mystery man was that people who knew what he actually looked like had an awkward habit of dying violently.

The Chinese's eyes had slitted further when the name slipped from the lips of his companion. "You fool," he hissed at the swarthy man. "You were warned never to use my name."

He looked back at me, his expression no longer amiable. "Now, Mr. Carter, your death is more certain than before."

"Your people must really want that device. They sure brought out the big artillery."

"No more small talk," he spat at me, furious that his companion had made a mistake. "You said you lied to us. Explain that to me."

"I did find the gadget. I have it in my pocket." I moved my hand. "I'll show it to you."

"Carter, move that hand again and I'll be checking the pockets of a dead man," Sheng said.

I froze. I knew he meant every word.

Sheng gestured. "Check his pockets," he told the man at the door.

The swarthy man moved forward and for an instant his body blocked Sheng's view, hiding the movement of my arm as I brought the stiletto sliding down into my palm.

He thrust his hand into my jacket pocket and as he did, I grasped Hugo and drove the razor sharp point into his fat belly. He gasped, his eyes bulging in pain. He slumped forward and I grabbed his shoulders to use him as a shield.

Sheng pumped a shot in my direction. It struck the swarthy man even as I caught hold of his sagging body. The impact caused him to jump even though the life was ebbing out of him before the bullet hit.

With gritted teeth, I gave the dead weight in my arms a backward shove, hurling the body toward the bunk and the Chinese agent. Sheng dodged. For a man of his size, he was remarkably fast. He got out of the way and the body of his companion slammed onto the bunk.

Sheng was about to fire again. I took a step toward him and heard the silencer-equipped revolver in his hand make its spitting sound. I bent, twisting my body forward and downward and kicking at him with my right foot.

His second shot missed because of my movement and then my kick, taught me by a Japanese master of karate, struck Sheng's gunhand brutally, cracking his fingers and sending the revolver flying from his grasp.

Before he could recover, I was moving toward him. I threw a fist at his pudgy face and caught him on the jaw. He gasped and staggered, but he was too strong to be kayoed with a single blow.

I reached into my jacket for Wilhelmina. I had my hand on the Luger's butt when the

Chinese surged back at me. He hit me squarely on the chin with a blow that almost snapped my neck and drove me against the bed.

Losing my balance, I fell on top of the motionless body of Sheng's companion. I rolled over and landed in a crouch on the floor and reached for the Luger again.

By this time, Sheng had opened the door. Astonishingly fast, he was into the corridor before I could point my gun in his direction.

I rose out of my crouch and dashed after him, shoving the half-open door out of my way. Sheng was not in sight. Grimly, I turned back to the Schmidt woman's compartment. There was a body there to be dealt with.

Pushing the door shut, I dragged the dead man to the window and dumped him out. I caught a glimpse of the body rolling down an incline before the train left it behind.

I was breathing heavily. I picked up the dead man's gun and found Sheng's weapon on the floor near the bunk. I threw them out, then closed the window and did a hasty job of tidying up the compartment. I didn't want the Schmidt woman to know I had been there.

My job was tougher now than it had been when I boarded the train. I had to find Sheng Tze. The encounter I'd just won didn't end it for us. I was the only free world agent still alive who knew what he looked like. He wasn't going to let me carry that knowledge around for long.

Five

I moved along the train from one end to the other and failed to spot the Chinese agent.

By the time I'd completed my search, the train had made two quick stops. Sheng Tze could have jumped off at either of them. He could also be aboard in one of the compartments I had been unable to enter, or in a dozen other places. I couldn't hope to explore all the places where a man could hide on a moving train.

I sighed and gave up for the moment. One way or the other, I was sure, I would be meeting Sheng again.

At mid-afternoon I found Ursula sitting alone in a day coach compartment. She was busy writing in a small notebook she had taken from her purse. I slid the compartment door open and entered.

"Hi," I said.

"Oh, Nick! Sit down. I was just trying to draft a note to my boss. I must tell him that so far I've come up empty-handed. I'll send a wire at Venice."

I sat down in a seat beside her. There were

three plush seats on each side of the compartment, each covered with a black-and-brown patterned material that gave it the look of a European tea room of the last century. The compartment dated back to the glamorous days of the train when kings and celebrities had taken the Orient Express. There were large and small luggage racks over the seats, a mirror on each wall, and photographs of scenes along the route flanking the mirrors.

Ursula put her notes away in her purse, and I caught a glimpse of a Webley .22 Lilliput automatic inside. I hoped she did not have to go up against her man with that tinkertoy. She looked over at me and the smile left her face.

"Nick! What happened to you?"

She was referring to the bruise that showed where Sheng had hit me. I grinned. "I've been practicing my profession."

"Are you all right?"

"Yes, I'm all right." It pleased me that she was genuinely concerned. "Say, there's no dining car on now, but I bought a bottle of bourbon at Milan. Would you like to join me in my compartment for a drink?"

She looked over at me with those cool blue eyes. She knew it was a proposition, and she knew I wanted her to know. She glanced back out at the moving countryside, which was flattening out now as we drew closer to the Adriatic.

"I think you are trying to seduce me, Nick."

"I am," I said.

She made a little face. "You haven't changed one bit. Can't you see I'm working?"

"You've got to relax sometime."

"It isn't easy to do that when you're tracking down a man like Hans Richter."

For the first time she had mentioned the name of the man she called the Butcher. I recognized it. I had read about Richter, and what I'd read hadn't been pretty.

"So he's the one you're after. I can understand your determination."

The door slid open, and a middle-aged woman stood there. "Are these seats taken?" she asked with a British accent, pointing to the four empty seats.

"No, please join us," Ursula said.

The woman came in and sat down at the window seat across from Ursula and me. She left the compartment door open, a cool breeze came in from the corridor. After she was seated, she reached into a straw bag for a bundle of knitting.

"It's a pleasant day," she smiled. She was a thin woman with a hawk nose and short gray hair. Her spectacles contained only the bottom part of the usual lens, small slivers of glass used for close-up work.

"Yes, isn't it?" Ursula agreed.

Ursula looked from the knitting to me and smiled. The woman went about her knitting busily, paying no further attention to us. I was just about to speak to Ursula again when a man came into the compartment. Without speaking to anyone, he sat down at the far end of the compartment, by the door. It was the man I had seen earlier with the radio, which he was still carrying. He set it down beside him on the seat, pulled a newspaper from under his arm, and began reading. Every time I had seen this man, he was carrying the radio, yet he never played it.

"Do you know when we arrive at Venice?" the British woman asked Ursula.

Ursula had been trying to get a better look at the man with the newspaper. She turned to the English lady now. "I expect around six or after."

"Oh, that isn't bad. We'll all have to get something to eat there, of course, since there's no dining car."

"Yes, that's right," Ursula said. I saw her face change, as if she had remembered something, and then she looked quickly back toward the man with the radio.

"I think it's terribly uncivilized not to send a dining car with us all the way," the British woman was saying.

Ursula was now staring at the man's left hand. I looked, too, and saw what she was looking at. The knuckle on the third finger of the hand that held the newspaper was large and gnarled. We exchanged glances. That knuckle was an identifying feature of Hans Richter.

Ursula could not get a good look at his face,

so I decided to help her. I waited until the man turned a page and then spoke to him.

"Excuse me, sir," I said.

The man dropped the newspaper to look at me. "Yes?" His accent was similar to Ursula's. He was about my height, and he had a military bearing. His muscular, intelligent face seemed younger, at first glance, than his years.

"I see you have a London paper," I said. "Are there any football scores in it?"

His gaze had drifted from me to Ursula and now came back to me again. He folded the paper and handed it across to me. "I'm sure there are. Here, I have just finished."

I avoided looking at his left hand. "Thanks," I said, taking the paper. I saw no scar on his neck.

He was looking at Ursula again. "It's all right." He picked up his radio and rose. "Now, if you will excuse me."

He turned and left the compartment, heading toward the sleeping cars. I turned to Ursula. "Well?"

"I don't know," she said.

The woman across the aisle stopped her knitting and listened to our conversation with open interest.

"There aren't many hands like that," I said.

"No," Ursula admitted. "Not many."

I stood. "I'll be back shortly."

I moved quickly down the corridor of the day

coach in the direction that the man had gone. I
caught up with him as he entered Voiture 5, the
car where the Topcon woman stayed. I stood at
the end of the car as he moved on. Then I
ducked around the corner of the corridor. In a
moment I heard a door close. He had gone into
Compartment 6.

While I was standing there, I made a decision.
My next move against Topcon would be less
subtle. I would have to go to Eva Schmidt and
ask her where the stolen device was hidden. Now
was as good a time as any. I knocked on the
door of Compartment 4, but there was no answer. I tried again, but all was quiet inside. I
would have to try later.

When I returned to Ursula, the woman was
still with her, discussing the merits of rail travel
over the airlines. Ursula looked relieved to see
me. "Let's take a walk," I said. "It's pleasant
out on the platforms."

"Don't forget to get something to eat at Venice," the woman said.

"We won't," I told her.

When we got into the corridor, I said, "Come
on, let's go to my compartment."

She gave me a look. "All right."

When we got to my compartment, which was
three down from Ursula's in the same car, I removed my jacket for comfort, and Ursula stared
at the big Luger in its holster. Then she shrugged
her thoughts away.

She sat warily on the edge of my bunk-bed while I broke out the bourbon and poured us each a drink. She took hers with a small smile. "Before you get me too drunk, tell me—did you locate the man with the radio?"

"He's in the next sleeper," I said. "Compartment 6. Do you think you've found the Butcher?"

"I saw no scar," she said.

"No. But his build is right, and his age."

"I don't know, I just don't know," she said slowly. "I have the feeling that the man is Richter, but I do not want to arrest the wrong person."

"Then you have only one alternative," I said. "You're going to have to try to find something in his personal effects that will make your identification more positive."

"Yes, you are right," she agreed. "I must try to get into his compartment."

I sighed. "Look, I'm an expert at this kind of thing. Let me search his compartment."

"You wouldn't know what to look for, Nick."

I thought a moment. "All right, we'll go together."

She smiled. "That's better. You can't have all the excitement."

I took a drink of the bourbon. "We can't go now," I said to her, moving my arm around her waist. "Richter, or whoever he is, just returned to the compartment. He'll be there for a while. We'll have to wait him out."

The blue eyes glanced at me, and she took a gulp of the bourbon. I took the cup from her hand and put it aside. I sat on the bunk's edge and pulled her to me. Then I planted a long kiss on her lips, and she responded. I kissed her neck under the blonde hair, and there was a little gasp from her throat. "Relax," I said.

By the time the next kiss was over, she had made up her mind to let me have her. I pulled her to her feet, and we began undressing without saying a word. Soon we were on the bunk, our bodies straining together. Lovely small sounds came from her throat. Her flesh was hot to my touch.

I slid my hands over her breasts. Ursula's eyes were closed. I saw her white teeth flash. She moaned and hooked her right arm around my neck. I felt her tremble and heard her gasp and then she fell back, a smile playing at the corners of her mouth.

The train wheels clacked away underneath us, and the car moved gently. It was a splendid moment, and neither of us was eager to break into it with words.

Finally, Ursula reached up and touched my cheek. "That was wonderful, Nick."

I smiled back at her. "It beats knitting in a day coach."

When we had dressed, I pulled the shade open

on the window. We were getting into the marshy country near Venice.

"Now, about that compartment we were going to search . . ." said Ursula.

"Let me check on your man and see if he is still there."

I eased into the corridor and moved along it to the compartment occupied by the man with the radio.

He opened the door just as I reached it and for a moment we gazed directly into each other's eyes. I kept walking and went past him to the end of the car. Then I turned and pretended to take a casual glance back. The man was still in the doorway and he was watching me.

Our eyes met again. His gaze was hard, challenging. Then he stepped back into the compartment and slammed the door.

The search I had suggested to Ursula was ruled out for the moment. Moreover, the man appeared suspicious of me. If he happened to be Hans Richter, that suspicion was understandable. To elude capture as long as Richter had, a man would have to be super-cautious, constantly watchful, distrustful of everyone. He probably slept with a gun near his hand.

Of course he was Richter, I thought. Ursula had to make absolutely sure because that was her job. She would need proof of his true identity in order to arrest him. But for all practical purposes, I was assuming that he was the Butcher of Belgrade. That malformed knuckle and the man's wary behavior had convinced me.

As I stood there at the end of the car, Eva Schmidt appeared, reminding me that I had a job of my own to do and that she appeared to be the key to it.

The woman brushed past me and I caught the scent of her perfume, which was very feminine. I looked at her legs as she moved on down the corridor. Not bad, I thought.

Pausing at the door of her compartment, she gave me the same appraising glance she had given me the first time I saw her. Then she unlocked the door and went in.

I returned to Ursula and told her the man I believed to be Richter was still in his quarters. "Try to keep a watch on his door. I have to see to a little business of my own," I said, making a check of the Luger.

"What sort of business, Nick?"

"Some people call it persuasion."

I knocked on Eva Schmidt's door and she opened it instantly. She looked surprised. "What do you want?" she asked in a German accent.

"In," I told her. I pushed her out of the way, then quickly closed the door behind me.

The woman eyed me warily, but she was definitely not on the edge of panic. "There are better ways to get acquainted," she said.

"This is more like a business call, Eva."

"If you are a policeman, I have nothing to hide.

If you are a thief, I have very little worth stealing."

"Only an electronic device any number of governments would like to have," I replied. "Let's not play around. I know you're a Topcon agent."

"What in the world is a Topcon agent?"

"I also know that you've been talking to a KGB agent. You're hoping to sell the device to the Soviets."

"What's a KGB agent?" she said. She was beginning to sound like a phonograph record.

I saw that I was going to have to convince her that I knew what I was talking about. I said, "I listened in on one of your conversations with the Russian. His name is Lubyanka. We have his picture in our files."

Her eyes narrowed. "And who are you, the CIA?"

"I'm in their line of work."

"Suppose I am trying to sell something to the Russians. How did you propose to stop me?"

"Well, there's one easy way. I can kill you."

Eva Schmidt didn't flinch. "Not on a crowded train, you can't. You're bluffing."

I moved my arm and the stiletto popped into my hand. "How very wrong you are. I've already killed one person on this train. I could easily make it two."

Her face paled and her eyes flicked nervously

to the knife's gleaming blade. "The monitor isn't in this compartment."

"Where is it?"

"I can't tell you that. If I did, my own people would kill me."

My hand darted toward her. With one swift movement, I sliced a button off the front of her dress and it popped to the floor and rolled.

"It could just as easily be your throat, Eva."

She gasped softly. Her eyes followed the button. "I don't have the device. I'm only handling negotiations with the Russian."

"The boss of Topcon is on the train, isn't he? You're a go-between, relaying the KGB's offers to him."

"Just a precaution. You know how it is. There's no one you can trust anymore." Apparently Eva Schmidt had a deadpan sense of humor.

I grinned at her and leaned against the compartment door. "If the KGB sets a price that's right, your boss comes out of the woodwork and turns over the monitor. Is that the plan?"

"You won't stop him from carrying it out. No one has ever stopped him."

"I specialize in firsts," I told her.

Then someone in the corridor turned the knob and gave the door a hard shove, throwing me off balance.

Eva Schmidt reacted as though she had been anticipating this opportunity. She lashed out with her foot and her heel caught me on the shin.

Driving a shoulder into my chest, she clamped both hands on my wrist and brought my arm down over her knee.

The woman had taken lessons from an expert. She would have snapped my arm if I hadn't moved with her, denying her the leverage she needed to offset my superior strength. I locked my free arm around her neck and yanked her head back so hard she grunted as though she'd been hit.

I brought the stiletto up and touched it to her throat, then spun around so that I was facing the door.

No one was there.

"Move again," I told Eva, "and this trip's over for you."

She stopped struggling. I watched the compartment door, which now hung ajar, tremble slightly with the motion of the train.

Dragging the woman with me, I checked the corridor. Eva's would-be caller had disappeared.

"You were expecting company. Who was it?" I asked her.

"The Russian. You scared him off."

I kicked the door shut. "I have a hunch you're lying and I just missed meeting Topcon's head man."

"If so, you're fortunate. He would have killed you."

That was the second time she'd told me how infallible the mystery man was. Either he aroused

a lot of admiration in his co-workers or Eva had
a personal interest in him. I remembered something the Chinese agent had said when he was
boasting. Eva was not the chief of Topcon but she
certainly wasn't just another hireling, he'd said.

"Tell me about your boy friend, Eva. Start
with his name."

"You're choking me. I can hardly talk."

I relaxed my hold a little and she repaid me
for the favor. She sank her teeth in my hand.

There are a few things you can't steel yourself
against. A deep bite from a keen set of teeth,
and Eva appeared to have the keenest, is one of
them.

I cursed and turned her loose.

The woman bounded away from me and
leaped for the knitting case I'd seen her carrying
in the day coach. She flipped the top back,
reaching inside.

I hit her with a flying tackle, waist-high. We
slammed onto the bunk. Eva kicked and
scratched my eyes. We rolled to the floor and her
knee flashed up and caught her target. I felt a
nauseating pain.

"Damn," I said. That was it. My patience had
run its course. I hit her with the flat of my hand
and her head struck the floor. I backhanded her
again and she cried out as blood trickled from
the corner of her lip.

I straddled her now, her bare thighs up against
my back. Her dress had been torn in the struggle

.and I could see part of one breast. Somehow she looked sexier than she had before, but I was in no mood for friendly games.

Eva put a hand to her mouth, then looked at the blood on it. "Donnerwetter!" she spat. But fear was strong in her eyes.

"If the idea occurred to you that I won't kill you because you're a woman, put it out of your head."

I held Hugo in front of her frightened eyes, then slid the blade up under her chin. "I won't threaten you again. I'll just do it."

"His name is Horst Blücher. I will tell you no more even if it means my life. I won't betray him. But if you wish to bid against the Russian for the device, I will get the word to Horst."

I thought about that for a moment. I had no authority to pay hard cash to get the device back, but Eva apparently meant it when she said she'd give up her life to protect her boss.

I reached over to the knitting case and dug into it and pulled out a Beretta. I tucked the automatic into my pocket just for insurance.

"You and this Horst must have a pretty cozy arrangement."

"He is a genius. I have great admiration for him."

"And a little more than that, I'll bet."

Eva touched the lip I'd cut with my backhand blow. "Yes, we're lovers. That's one of the reasons I'd die for him."

"My government might be willing to make an offer to get the monitor back. Get the message to your man."

"I will see what he says."

"When will I know?"

"I suppose I can have an answer by tonight."

I got off her and she sat up and leaned heavily against the side of the bunk. I felt there was little chance Horst would take the bait and come out into the open. But I was taking a long shot, hoping Eva would lead me to him.

Outside in the corridor, I wondered if I had made a mistake. There was a possibility Eva would succeed in contacting Horst without my knowledge and he would simply set out to polish me off. Then I'd have both Topcon's big gun and the Chinese killer after my scalp. That was not a prospect I found appealing.

Six

Ursula was gone.

I had left her watching the door of the man we suspected of being Hans Richter, the Nazi war criminal called the Butcher. She was not at the end of the car where I had seen her last, and she was neither in her own compartment nor in mine.

A girl as singleminded as Ursula wouldn't have left her post without good reason, I thought. She must have seen the man leave his compartment and decided to follow him.

Stopping before the man's door, I knocked. I drew no response. I glanced along the corridor. A traveler had entered the car and was moving toward me with a smile on his face. Where had I seen him before? Then I remembered. Earlier in the journey, he had been seated in the same day car as Eva Schmidt and the man we believed to be Richter.

He greeted me cheerfully. "How is the trip going?" When I told him it was going fine, he nodded and clapped me on the shoulder in a comradely gesture, then moved on.

I lingered, waiting for him to get out of sight. I was going into the compartment while no one was there and conduct the search Ursula had wanted. The sooner she got her business settled, the sooner I would stop feeling responsible for her.

The cheerful stranger had stopped. He turned around. "May I ask you a question?"

"Yes."

He moved the hand that was in the pocket of his jacket. "Would you believe me if I said I was holding a revolver?"

"I don't know why you'd lie to me about a thing like that." I was impressed by his acting ability. He looked every inch a jovial tourist. He even wore a camera on a strap around his neck.

"I am going to take you to someone who wishes to talk to you. That is all we want, a little talk," he said.

"Then the gun isn't necessary."

"Perhaps not, but I prefer to be careful. I'll walk a short distance behind you. Close enough to shoot, but not close enough for you to jump me. If you behave yourself, we will get along splendidly."

"I try to get along with everyone," I said. "Where are we going?"

"Just turn and start walking. I'll tell you when to stop."

I behaved myself and followed orders. I was interested in learning who had sent him after me.

"All right. Stop," he said after we had moved into the adjoining car.

I paused without looking back. We were alongside a row of private compartments. I heard the jovial man turn a key in a lock.

"Now you may turn around and step inside," he said.

I followed orders until I got inside the compartment. Then I saw Ursula and I went a little crazy.

The girl was lying on top of the bunk. She was completely nude. Her clothing had been stripped from her and scattered about the compartment. She was breathing, but she was motionless.

Disregarding the gun, I wheeled on my captor. I leaped for him. My hands closed on his throat. I slammed him against the compartment wall, choking him. "What did you do to her?"

Then the door behind me opened. I heard it, but I didn't turn in time. A leaded sap struck me behind the ear and floored me.

I tried to get up and couldn't. I felt my hands being drawn behind me. Then someone was trussing my wrists with silken cord, yanking the bonds tight with smooth efficiency.

A hand slapped my shoulder. The man who had straddled me to do the tying job said, "Do not worry about the girl. She was only knocked out."

I recognized the voice as that of the jovial tourist.

My hazed vision began to clear. I saw the feet of another man who was standing near the door. He wore expensive black leather shoes. Apparently he was the one who had sapped me. "Find out who he is," he said to Mr. Cheerful.

Then he stepped out of the door before I had a chance to get a look at his face.

When the door closed behind the man with the black shoes, Mr. Cheerful turned me over. He was still beaming like the chairman of a welcoming committee. "As I said before, you won't be killed if you behave yourself."

"What about the girl?"

"I understand your concern. She is a pretty thing. But we had to find out who she is. So I knocked her out and took off her clothes and went through them."

"How much did you find out?"

"Her organization issues identification cards to its agents. Naturally she was carrying one."

That was the trouble with being connected with Ursula's kind of undercover policy agency. They adhered to all the bureaucratic habits that could be dangerous to an operative out in the field.

"Do you, too, have an identification card?" asked the cheerful man.

"No," I said.

I hoped that if I kept him talking long enough, I could get him within range of a skillfully placed kick. Then I could start a whole new ballgame, with me pitching.

"The two of you have been prowling the train together, trying doors, peeking into other people's compartments. If you don't work as partners, how do you explain that?"

"Hell," I said, "Can't you figure out anything for yourself?"

"No, I'm lazy." He extracted another piece of cord from his pocket. "I'm going to make it hard for you to move around." He deftly looped my ankles with the cord, taking pains to see that I didn't catch him off guard. I had no chance for a well-placed kick.

In the corridor, the man had shown the same caution, undoubtedly born of experience. Whoever he was, he knew the rules of the game.

Mr. Cheerful's accent was German, like Eva Schmidt's. Like Ursula's, for that matter. It was not much of a clue to his allegiance. In the spy business, sides get switched quite often, professionals of all nationalities were available for hire to any client, and what appeared obvious frequently turned out to be a false lead.

The assistant to Sheng Tze, for example, had been about as Chinese as Frank Sinatra.

As far as I knew, Mr. Cheerful could be working for anyone from Topcon to East German intelligence. He could also be a pal of Hans Richter, the man Ursula had been assigned to apprehend.

I could only be certain that he wasn't working for AXE, for reasons that were perfectly clear, or for Peking. If he were employed by the Chinese Communists, Sheng Tze would be present and I would probably be dead already.

He dropped my feet, then gave them a little jerk to test the strength of his work. Satisfied, he straightened up. "Now that we're comfortable, we can talk. Tell me all about yourself."

"From the beginning? Well, I was born in the United States of America . . ."

"You joke too much," he warned me.

He walked over to the bed and gazed down at the nude Ursula, who was bound hand and foot with the same kind of cord that held me. He glanced up to make sure I was watching his every move, then deliberately flicked one of the unconscious girl's nipples with his fingernail.

"I am not going to try to beat answers out of you. It would be too difficult. If you don't tell me who you are, I'll work on the girl."

I couldn't see what I had to gain by withholding the information. "I take my orders from an organization called AXE. My name is Nick Carter."

"Your name and that of your organization are familiar to me. But I do not understand why you and the girl are working together."

"Maybe you won't believe this, but we just happen to be old friends who were taking the same train."

"The girl hunts down former Nazis. Are you hunting a former Nazi, too?"

"Not exactly. But if I run into one, I sure won't kiss him on both cheeks."

"I would imagine not, Mr. Carter. In any event, I have to be going." He glanced at his watch, then walked quickly to the door. "Enjoy the rest of your trip."

I watched the door close and heard the lock click. Then the compartment was silent. I glanced around. There was no luggage or clothing to indicate that the quarters were occupied by a passenger. Maybe Mr. Cheerful had a master key and had picked an empty sleeper in which to hold us prisoner.

I was surprised that he had asked his questions and then left us unharmed. But I wasn't about to complain. My problem was to get us out of here.

"Ursula," I said. "Wake up, Ursula."

The girl didn't move. I wriggled over to the bunk, my progress slow and awkward. Then I got up on my knees and spoke to Ursula again. Her eyelashes fluttered slightly.

She was a pretty picture, fresh and inviting. I leaned over and touched her nipple with my tongue. It was one way of waking her up.

Ursula smiled instinctively. Then she stirred on the bunk. Her eyes flew open. "Nick!"

"Surprise," I said.

I tongued the nipple again. I hated to stop.

"This is no time for that," she chided me. "How did you get here?"

"A stocky man brought me. A cheerful fellow with a camera hanging around his neck. What's your side of the story?"

"I was watching the compartment in Voiture 5 while you went about your business, whatever it was. The man came out. Carrying that blasted radio of his as usual. He was in such a hurry that I was sure he was going to meet someone. I decided to follow and see what it was that he felt was so urgent. He must have spotted me. He led me through the day coach where that cheerful fellow, the one with the camera, was sitting. They must have exchanged signals in some way. The two of them trapped me out on the platform. I was forced to come here. Then I was slugged behind the ear."

"I see a lovely little goose egg there, but you're in fine shape just the same."

Ursula blushed a little. "You have me at a definite disadvantage."

"I wish I could figure out a way to capitalize on it."

"Try to keep your mind on business. What do we do next?"

"I'll think of something," I assured her.

Already my mind was reviewing the events of the afternoon. Something didn't fall into place and I was annoyed that I couldn't pin it down.

I tried to arrange the conclusions I'd reached

in a logical order. The man with the radio was Richter, Ursula's fugitive Nazi. He had a malformed knuckle like Richter and his behavior was that of a man accustomed to being on the run. After he got wise to Ursula, it was only natural that he would try to find out who I was. He had seen me with the German girl.

Richter had slugged me as I struggled with his confederate, Mr. Cheerful. He was the man who'd told Mr. Cheerful to determine my identity. But why would a man as careful as Richter leave the questioning to a companion? For that matter, why was Richter traveling with a companion who appeared to be a skilled agent? Maybe Herr Richter was in the spy business these days.

"Move over, Ursula, and make room for me. I'm going to get on the bed with you," I said.

"Nick!" she scolded. "Not now."

"You misunderstand, baby. I'm going to get on the bed so I can try to untie your hands."

We sat back to back and I worked at the tight knots in the cords that bound her. The task was so difficult I cursed Mr. Cheerful a half-dozen times.

"Nick, why did they take off my clothes?"

"Not just for the view, lovely though it is. Mr. Cheerful wanted to search your clothing."

"Did anything, well, happen while I was knocked out?"

"Nothing you'd have minded missing," I grinned.

As I worked at the knots in the cord, my hands occasionally brushed against Ursula's naked back and buttocks. "There are some fringe benefits to this job," I told her.

"Did they find anything when they searched me, Nick?"

"Your ID card. Richter knows who you are."

At that moment, I saw Mr. Cheerful's camera. He had left it behind in the compartment.

"What's the matter?" asked Ursula.

"He left his camera."

"You mean he may be coming back for it?"

"Not on your life," I said. "A man that careful doesn't forget something like a camera."

Not unless he intended to forget it.

I wormed off the bed and dropped to the floor. I rolled to the camera because that was the fastest way to get there.

"Ursula, get off the bed and put your back to the window and raise it." I said.

She had her wits about her. From my tone of voice, she knew she shouldn't waste time. I heard her bare feet hit the floor.

I lay on my stomach and examined the camera at close range. If I was right, I was risking getting a blast right in the face, but that couldn't be helped.

"I can't see any timing device and I can't hear

a ticking, but I think there's an explosive device inside."

"The man left it behind on purpose?" said Ursula. She was at the window now.

"Having found out who you are, why should Hans Richter leave you alive? This compartment is supposed to become our tomb, baby."

I heard Ursula breathing hard. She was getting hold of the window, yanking it up.

"Mr. Cheerful looked at his watch before he left us. I've got to assume he activated the timing device by pushing down the lever on the camera. I may set it off if I pick up the camera, but I've got to take the chance."

I turned my back to the camera and grabbed hold of it with both hands. I was sweating. I didn't tell Ursula, but I figured that if the explosive did go off when I moved the camera, at least my body would shield part of the blast and perhaps save her life.

"Move away from the window," I told her.

She spoke my name in a soft voice and then she moved, and I stood up.

No explosion.

I hopped toward the train window. I didn't want to take the risks involved in rolling across the floor. I turned my back to the window and leaned against it and gave the camera a flip with my tied hands.

The train churned onward and I looked at Ur-

sula and we smiled at each other, our relief
showing.

Then we heard the explosion back along the
tracks. It sounded like a hand grenade going off
on the other side of a hill.

"I'm glad you saw that camera when you
did," Ursula said.

"Yeah, a few minutes more and we'd have
been finished."

"I'm sorry, Nick. Because of me, your life is
in danger. Richter will be out to get both of us
now."

Ursula saw only the tip of the iceberg. Hans
Richter and his lieutenant, Mr. Cheerful, were
but a minority among the killers riding this
train.

Seven

I managed to free Ursula's hands by the time the Orient Express stopped at Venice. She got rid of the cords around her ankles and donned a couple of key pieces of clothing before she unbound me.

"Don't be shy," I teased her. "By now I know everything about you."

"No, Nick. You only know what I look like. A man never knows everything about a woman."

We left the compartment and mingled with the crowd leaving the train. Ursula dashed for sandwiches while I took up a post that permitted me to watch for the faces that meant something to the two of us.

I didn't see Hans Richter and his companion and I didn't spot Sheng Tze, the Chinese Communist agent. I did catch a glimpse of Eva Schmidt. Like Ursula, she was picking up sandwiches.

"Eva," I called as she passed me, headed back for the train with a bag of food in her hand.

She paused. "You gave me until tonight, remember?"

"Just checking in, that's all."

"I will make contact with Horst and relay your message about being interested in the monitor. But I won't make that contact until I'm sure the moment is right. In other words, I have no intention of giving his identity away to you or to anyone else who might be watching me."

Then she drifted off with the crowd and I turned my attention to Ursula, who had come up behind me with our sandwiches.

"I thought you were trying to pick up another playmate," she said, "until I heard a bit of your conversation. Who is Horst?"

"Just a man I want to meet. You keep your mind on Richter, baby."

Soon the Orient Express was pulling out of the station, going in the direction that it had come. In order to head east again, the train had to return to the mainland across a causeway. Dark was falling as the Express churned along the two miles of causeway and we saw behind us a dazzling display of yellow lights along the shoreline: the lights of Venice rising out of the blackness of the sea.

After a quick meal, Ursula said she wanted to take another crack at Hans Richter. "Let's try his compartment. If he's there, I'll arrest him. If he isn't, we'll make a search of his belongings and find out what he's up to."

Richter wasn't there and I wasn't surprised.

"By now he knows that we weren't killed.

There should have been an explosion that never took place."

"Nick, do you think I've lost him?"

"He didn't get off the train at Milan," I pointed out.

I picked the lock and we entered the Butcher's compartment.

I switched on the overhead light. There were two pieces of luggage, both on the floor instead of on the racks. I took one, and Ursula reached for the other. After we picked the locks on the cases, we opened them carefully.

There was nothing of significance in the bag that I searched, but there was a handkerchief that surely did not belong to the man who had the radio. It had a slight scent of perfume, and the scent seemed vaguely familiar to me. I closed the bag and helped Ursula look through the other one. A moment later, she held up a piece of paper.

"Look at this," she said. "He plans to get off at Belgrade." It was his train ticket.

I grunted. "That doesn't give you much time."

I poked into a corner of the case, underneath some shirts, and found a couple of packs of European cigarettes. They appeared to be a custom blend. "Expensive taste," I noted, holding one of the packs up for Ursula to see.

She took the cigarettes from me and looked at

the package. "Hans Richter smoked a special brand of Belgian cigarette. This is that brand."

"You'll have to try to grab him at Belgrade, when he gets off the train."

"The Yugoslav authorities have promised to help bring Richter to justice. I will have them meet us at the station with a couple of plain-clothes policemen."

"Wouldn't you rather make the arrest alone?" I asked.

"He must be captured alive," she said. "If I get that Nazi pig alone I'm afraid I'll blow his brains out."

We put everything back just the way it was and left the compartment. Ursula went to her compartment to draft a wire while I took a walk through the rumbling train.

We had made our stop at Trieste just after Venice. By nine-thirty we were due at Poggiore-ale del Corsa on the Yugoslav border. I decided that if Eva Schmidt had not contacted me by then, I would start looking for her.

I returned to my compartment in the hope that Eva would get in touch with me there. I had given her its number when she promised to tell Horst Blücher I wanted in on the bidding for the satellite monitor.

Company was waiting for me, but it wasn't Eva Schmidt or her boy friend. Ivan Lubyanka, the KGB man, reclined on my bunk, his left hand pillowing his head. In his right hand he held a Webley .455 Mark IV revolver with silencer.

"Come in," he said.

I closed the door behind me, thinking that I should have been more careful.

Lubyanka sat up on the bunk. "So you are Nick Carter. You don't look so tough."

"Who told you I was tough? I'm a pussycat."

"If I had realized you were traveling on the train with me, Carter, I'd have dropped in to see you sooner."

I grunted. "If you had been doing your homework, you'd have recognized me when you saw me in the dining car. I recognized you."

He studied me petulantly. "You know, of course, that I must kill you."

I hunched my shoulders. "Why bother?" I asked. "You'll probably outbid me anyway."

"I did not come here to bid," he said flatly with a thick accent. "I came here as the only purchaser, and I want it to remain that way."

"What about the Chinese?"

"I will deal with one competitor at a time," he answered smoothly.

"If you do, you'll have bodies all over this train. You ought to think about that." I didn't bother trying for Hugo because I knew Lubyanka would not give me time.

"I have thought about it," he said. He rose from the bunk. He stood a couple inches shorter than me, and I could see that he did not like that very much. "You and I are moving down to the end of this train, Carter. We are walking very carefully. I will hold this gun in my pocket on the way, but it will be aimed at your spine. As you know, a spinal shot is very painful. So I hope you will not do anything foolish."

"And what happens at the end of our nice walk together?"

"Don't worry, it will be very quick."

"How generous of you."

"Please. You will go with me now." He waved the big gun at me, and I realized that if that thing went off, it would make a hole in my middle big enough for a man to jam his fist into.

I turned and opened the door, hoping there was somebody in the corridor. There was not. I entered the corridor, and Lubyanka followed right behind me. The gun was still held out in front of him but as I watched, he stuck it into a jacket pocket. I could see the muzzle protruding under the cloth, aimed at my waist.

He closed the compartment door and nodded for me to start walking. I turned and moved slowly down the corridor ahead of him. The train rumbled and rocked under us, but not enough to disturb Lubyanka's balance. He kept about three paces between us, so that I could not get to him easily.

We arrived at the end of Voiture 7 and moved out on the platforms between it and 5, where Eva Schmidt's compartment was located. We had to pass through two sets of doors. As I passed through the second set, Lubyanka right behind me, I made my move.

I slammed the door back against Lubyanka with a violent motion. The door struck him and knocked him off balance, and he fell to the floor of the platform. But he didn't lose the revolver. He fired as he fell. The first slug smashed glass in the door, passed through it, and narrowly missed my shoulder, burying itself in the wood paneling behind me. A second shot rang out, but it didn't even come close.

As Lubyanka scuttled for position on the platform, I yanked Wilhelmina free. My shot hit the metal floor of the platform just beside the crouching Russian, ricocheting around him without hitting him.

Lubyanka fired again, chipping the door frame that I was using for cover. Then, while I was ducking back behind my door, he scurried back through the door of the other car. I saw him at the last minute and managed to squeeze off two more shots from the Luger. One slug tore into Lubyanka's shoulder, and I could see him drop to the floor in the other car.

There was a long, empty moment as the wheels clattered loudly beneath us. Then I saw a raised hand holding a revolver. Lubyanka fired a quick shot at me, but it went wild. Next I saw his head darting along the bottom of the window. I fired at it but missed. Then he was gone, running down

the corridor that led to the other end of the car.
He had probably decided to go off and lick his
wounds.

I moved cautiously out on my side of the platform and quickly crossed over the gap to a position beside the other door. No more shots came.
I peeked inside, but Lubyanka was nowhere in
sight. Perhaps he was setting a trap for me in
there.

I opened the door a crack to get a better look.
Nothing. It looked as if Lubyanka had really
left. I slowly entered the car, holding the Luger
out in front of me. He wasn't there. Then I
rounded the corner and saw him about two-
thirds of the way down the corridor. He turned,
his face dark with anger and frustration, and
fired two unsteady shots from his reloaded
revolver. I crouched quickly and the slugs whined
over my head.

I swore under my breath. Just as Lubyanka
was turning to run down the rest of the corridor,
I took another shot at him. But the train's
movement spoiled my aim, and I narrowly missed
him. Then the Russian disappeared around the
corner, on his way out of the car.

Apparently no one had heard the exchange of
muffled shots. No one came out of the compartments. As I reached the end of the car and the
spot where the KGB man had dissappeared from
my view, I saw that the train was pulling into
Poggioreale del Corsa.

Lubyanka would not get off at this quick stop, I told myself. He would not want the authorities to discover that he was wounded. He was in no position to explain what had happened. Besides, he still wanted the monitor he was trying to buy from the Topcon agents aboard the train.

A pair of uniformed men came down the corridor toward me. One was a train conductor, the other a customs man. We were near the border and were being checked.

I produced the false identification which AXE's special division had provided. The customs man nodded and he and the conductor moved on.

The train picked up speed, moving at a steady clip into Yugosalvia. The next stop would be around midnight at Pivka.

My next item of business, I thought, was to pay a visit to Eva Schmidt. The woman had to be the one who had told Lubyanka I was trying to get my hands on the satellite monitor.

I tried Eva's compartment, but she wasn't there. Once again I picked the lock and entered with the Luger in my hand. No one was there. It figured that since her compartment was the only one I could identify by number my adversaries would hold conferences elsewhere.

I left the compartment and walked back toward the day coaches, looking all the while for Lubyanka and Schmidt—and looking for Sheng, too, since I had reason to think that he was still aboard and after my hide.

My search was fruitless. There was no sign of any of them. I began to worry that maybe they had all somehow gotten off at the border.

Then the train was pulling into the Pivka station. Pivka is just a country town that happens to be situated where several Yugoslav railway lines meet. The station is a primitive one—a long gray building that shows few lights at night. It was cold there in the mountains. There was a drizzling rain as the train stopped at the station.

I watched from one of the car platforms to see if anybody would get off. Four people appeared on the platform. Three of them were passengers who had decided to get a snack at the sandwich and coffee shop in the near end of the station building. The fourth, whom I finally recognized by his familiar gait, was Ivan Lubyanka.

Without glancing once over his shoulder, Lubyanka hurried through the station building to a dark street beyond. I hesitated for a moment. This could be a ruse to distract my attention while Schmidt and Blücher left from another car. But I had to take that chance. I stepped to the ground and started after Lubyanka. He just might have the stolen monitor.

Lubyanka had already disappeared into the gray building. I hurried after him, hoping the train wouldn't pull out before I could get back. The dimly lighted, shabby waiting room was almost empty. Lubyanka wasn't there—he must have already left the building.

I ran through the doorway to the street and looked up and down the dark sidewalk outside. The light rain wet my face—it was a cold, miserable night. There were no automobiles or pedestrians anywhere in sight—just gray stone fences, gray buildings, and the rain. Lubyanka had completely disappeared.

I had to decide whether to go after Lubyanka and forget the train and Schmidt and Blücher or to get back aboard on the chance that they were still there with the stolen device.

It was a pressure decision because I was running out of time—that train was due to leave in ten or fifteen minutes. If I made the wrong decision, I'd be back where I started in my search for the monitor, and I might even lose it for good.

In a moment I had chosen. I turned on my heel and hurried back through the dimly lighted station to the platform. The lights on the Orient Express were strung out along the track before me. The train looked like an oasis of civilization in this black wilderness. I gazed toward the restaurant and saw a few people inside, huddled over cups of hot coffee or tea at rough wood tables. A Yugoslav child who should have been in bed at that hour was moving to a table with a cup of steaming tea. He wore a white apron and highly polished patent leather shoes. After I had surveyed the faces of the customers and was sure that none of them was familiar to me, I headed for the men's room. As I relieved myself, I wondered where Lubyanka had gone and whether he intended to consummate the deal for the monitor.

As I turned to leave, I noticed a man standing in the doorway—my old friend Sheng Tze. He was grinning slightly, and he was holding a revolver in his right hand. It was a Smith & Wesson .44 Magnum with a big silencer.

"We meet for the last time, Mr. Carter," Sheng said. "Our Russian friend has conveniently left the train, and when I dispose of you, I will have no other competitors."

I watched the gun and his gun hand. "There is still Blücher himself to deal with." I noticed that the only light in the room came from a dim bulb that hung from the ceiling, only a short distance from where I stood. But I saw no way to darken the place without getting two or three slugs in me. And the room offered absolutely no cover of any kind.

"The woman will be my way to the device," Sheng said coolly. "But that will be my problem, not yours." He raised the gun slightly; and it was aimed at my heart. Just as he was about to squeeze the trigger, a man walked through the door behind him. He was a Yugoslav, a station official.

"What is this?" he asked, looking at Sheng's long pistol.

He was standing within three feet of Sheng. Sheng twisted around toward him, threw his left elbow out and smashed it into his face. There was a dull crunching sound and a muffled cry, and the fellow slumped to the floor, unconscious.

But I did not wait for the official to hit the floor. Before Sheng could turn back to finish me off, I grabbed at the string on the small light bulb in front of me and yanked hard as I spun off to my left.

The room was plunged into almost total darkness, the only dim light coming from the station platform through the open door. Sheng fired in my direction but missed by a foot. The gun popped dully in the room, and the slug chewed into the cement wall behind me. As I turned around to face Sheng again, he was taking aim. I hurled the stiletto through the darkened room, and it struck Sheng in the forearm above the hand holding the revolver. The hand opened spasmodically, and the gun flew across the room.

Sheng uttered a loud cry as he stared at the knife imbedded in his forearm, which had severed tendon, arteries, and muscle. He turned, the knife still in his arm, to look for his gun. Then he took a step toward it, but I blocked him. He swore in Chinese.

"No more guns, Sheng," I said in a low growl. "Let's see what you can do without them."

Sheng hesitated a moment, then pulled the stiletto from his forearm with a grunt of pain.

Blood gushed to the floor. He grabbed the handle of the knife expertly with his left hand, and started toward me.

I could have tried to reach for the gun on the floor, but I knew I'd never get to it before Sheng. As for Wilhelmina, my Luger would have sounded like a cannon in that station.

Sheng was now circling me. I had to retreat from his gun on the floor. He couldn't get to it, either, but he was perfectly content with his new advantage. He expected to cut me to shreds with the stiletto.

Sheng stepped in quickly, feinting with the knife. He was good with it. I avoided a quick hard thrust, but a second assault cut through my jacket sleeve and scratched my arm. The grin was returning to his broad face. He was confident. He made another swipe with the blade and gashed my chest.

Our eyes were adjusting to the dimness now, and I could see the blood dripping steadily from Sheng's right forearm as he methodically stalked me in a tight circle. He saw the blood on my shirt, too, and his face showed he liked what he saw. He figured it would just be a matter of seconds till he could finish me off.

Then Sheng made his big move. He came in for the kill with a thrust at my belly. I stepped and twisted to one side and chopped down at his wrist with my right hand. I hit him solidly, and the arm was jarred under the impact. Hugo clattered to the floor.

Before Sheng could recover, I turned closer to him and chopped down on his head and neck with the heel of my hand. He grunted and slipped to his hands and knees. I stepped over him to deliver another blow, but he was ready for me. He kicked out with his right foot and knocked me down with a blow on my upper leg.

We both scrambled to our feet at the same time, but I had the edge on him because I was not hurt as badly. I threw a fist at him, but he saw it coming in the nick of time. Despite his bad arm, he grabbed me and threw me over his shoulder in a wide arc. I saw ceiling and floor as I reached for him on the way down. I landed on one knee, still holding on to him. With the momentum he had created, I swung him over my back, turning him upside down in the air and landing him hard on his back on the concrete floor. He hit with a loud thud, and I could hear the air punched from his lungs.

I regained my footing as Sheng, out of breath, struggled weakly to his knees. Then I kicked out savagely at his head, and he fell to his side. He tried to make it to his knees again, but I was waiting for him. Just as he struggled weakly to his feet, I took careful aim, chopped down hard with the back of my hand at the bridge of his nose, and connected with a loud crack. Sheng grunted and hit the floor flat on his back. Then he twitched twice and was dead.

I glanced out of the door and saw that the conductors were preparing to start the Orient Express again. After I retrieved Hugo and Wilhelmina, I buttoned my jacket to cover the blood on my shirt, and rushed into the rainy night to the train.

Eight

Soon after the train departed from Pivka, I found Ursula on the rear platform, alone, checking out the ammunition in her Webley Lilliput. She was relieved to see me.

"I saw you get off, and I thought you might have run into trouble at the station," she said.

I had changed my jacket and shirt so there was no evidence of my run-in with Sheng. "There have been a few developments for me," I admitted. "Getting ready for Belgrade?"

She smiled a tense smile. "Yes. I am a little anxious about it, I guess."

"Well, it's almost one o'clock. I suggest you go get some sleep. We don't arrive at Belgrade until nine A.M."

"I will get some rest," she said. "I promise."

"Good. I have a little something to do. I'll see you early tomorrow morning. Are you heading back to your compartment?"

"I think I'll get some air first," she said. She leaned over and touched my lips with hers. *"Dankeschön* for worrying about me, Nick."

I smiled. "See you later."

110

I left Ursula on the platform and walked back through Voiture 7, now the last coach, toward 5, where I hoped to find Eva Schmidt.

I had reached the far end of Voiture 7, when I saw a man headed toward me through the corridor of the next sleeper. It was Hans Richter. He was no longer carrying the radio with him, and his face looked very businesslike. I ducked back out of sight and ran ahead of him, back to my compartment. I unlocked the door and got inside just as Richter rounded the corner of the corridor.

I waited until I heard him pass before stepping back out into the corridor behind him. He was headed toward Ursula who was still on the rear platform. At first I thought it was probably just a coincidence, but then I saw him stop at the end of the corridor, remove a big stiletto knife from his pocket, and snick the blade open. There was little doubt about it: he knew Ursula was there. Apparently he had guessed that she was after him, and was going to kill her.

Richter disappeared around the corner of the corridor. I moved quickly after him, realizing that it would take only a moment for him to kill Ursula if she hadn't seen him coming and that the clatter of the train would cover any sound he made.

It took me just a moment to round the corner of the corridor and reach the platform door. When I looked through it, I saw that Richter had already grabbed Ursula from behind and was holding the knife at her throat. His other hand was over her mouth, and I could imagine her very wide, fear-glazed eyes.

Richter was speaking to his captive in an arrogant, hard voice, as I eased the door open behind him.

"Yes, I know it's unpleasant to die. But that is what the Bonn government has in mind for me, isn't it?"

It was a tricky situation. I could not just kill Hans Richter because Ursula and Bonn wanted him alive. It was important to them that he suffer the ignominy of public trial.

I eased the door shut behind me, pulled out Wilhelmina, and moved up behind Richter just as he was about to draw the stiletto across Ursula's throat. Then I placed the muzzle of the automatic up against the base of Richter's skull so he could feel it there.

Richter turned his head quickly, still holding the knife to Ursula's neck. When he saw me behind him, a look of pure hatred came into his hard, muscular face.

"You?" he exclaimed.

"You had better drop the knife," I said, nuzzling the Luger up tightly against his skull.

"And what if I do not?"

"Then I'll blow your face off," I said grimly, hoping he did not call the bluff.

"Not before I am able to open up this lady's

throat like a ripe tomato. No, I have the advantage here, my friend. If you do not put your gun away immediately, and leave this platform, I will kill her instantly.

"You misunderstand my motive for being here," he continued smoothly. "I only intended to frighten the lady off. I was not going to actually kill her. Nor will I kill her now if you leave this platform. If you do not, however, I will be forced to sever her jugular."

Richter was a smooth liar, but not a convincing one. I knew that if I left the platform, I would not see Ursula alive again.

I saw blue eyes look toward me in desperation. I swallowed hard and shoved the Luger even tighter against the base of his skull.

"All right," I said, "do it."

Richter glanced at me. "You mean you will let me kill her?"

"That's right," I said. "After that, the front of your head will disappear into the blackness out there. Now you decide, Richter. Drop the knife or you're dead."

I hoped I sounded convincing. Richter hesitated a moment, thinking it out, evaluating. Then I saw his face change and relax a little. He took the knife from Ursula's throat and dropped his other hand from her mouth.

I took a long step away from Richter, and he moved slightly away from Ursula. She turned toward him now, breathing hard.

"Well, it appears that you finally have me," he said to Ursula in a sarcastic tone. *"Wie schade für mich."* Too bad for him—his sarcasm heavier than ever.

"It looks as if we've made ourselves an arrest earlier than you had wanted," I said to Ursula, not taking my eyes off Richter.

"We will take him to my compartment. I will guard him all night so that he does not break free," Ursula said.

Richter grunted a small laugh.

"All right," I said. I did not like having this man on our hands until morning, particularly while I was worrying about Eva Schmidt and Blücher, but there was no other choice. "Move, Richter." I waved the Luger toward the platform door.

He still had the knife in his hand, and I reached out to take it from him as he passed me. He gave it to me without trouble, but then as I threw it overboard, taking my eyes from him for just a split-second, he jammed a hand at my right wrist and pushed the Luger away from him.

We slammed up against the bulkhead together, Richter twisting to grab at the gun. At one point I might have taken the chance of firing at him, but Ursula was standing in the line of fire behind him.

I turned with Richter, as I spun him in a small circle until his back slammed up against the rear of the train. Ursula was no longer behind him. I was fighting to turn the Luger in toward him. I no longer cared if I killed Richter or not, but I would try instead to wound him. Grunting and sweating, I forced the muzzle of the automatic toward his body. He squeezed my hand, and a shot was fired from the Luger. The slug hit the bulkhead and ricocheted into the night.

Ursula had just gotten her Webley out, but I was between her and Richter, and she could not use it against him. In a sudden vicious and desperate thrust, Richter threw me away from him. I fell against Ursula momentarily, knocking the Webley from her grasp. Then Richter started through the door. It closed behind him as I fired another shot from the Luger. The slug shattered glass and hit him as he moved around the corner toward the corridor. The impact of the slug slammed him against the wall. But he was still on his feet. Then he disappeared from view.

"Damn!" I shouted. "Are you all right?"

Ursula was retrieving her Webley. "I'm okay, Nick," she said, but I could see she was shaken.

I grabbed at the door, pulled it open, and entered the sleeping car. As I rounded the corner of the corridor with the Luger still in hand, I saw Richter about halfway down, running toward the other end. I leveled the Luger at him but then I thought better of it. Most of the passengers were in bed in their compartments now, and a shot would be sure to wake them up.

I dropped the Luger and watched Richter disappear through the other end of the car. Ursula was now beside me.

"Sorry," I said to her.

"Don't worry, Nick. He is still on the train. Next time, he won't be so lucky. We'll make sure of that. Shall we look for him?"

"Let's."

We went to Richter's compartment, but he wasn't there. Then we searched the rest of the train. He was nowhere in sight. He had evidently found a place to hide. It looked as if we would have to count on Ursula's being able to grab him at Belgrade in the morning. I insisted that Ursula go to her compartment for a short rest. She needed it badly. I drifted back toward Voiture 5, hoping to make contact with the Schmidt woman.

When I arrived at Voiture 5, I had a big surprise awaiting.

I had just started into the corridor toward Eva's compartment when her door opened and Hans Richter appeared.

I ducked around the corner and watched. He was shrugging into his jacket and there was a bandage on his arm. He looked around furtively and then headed away from me, toward the day coaches.

From all appearances, the ex-Nazi had hidden in the Schmidt woman's compartment while we were looking for him. He'd also acquired a bandage, which meant Eva must have helped him.

"Richter!" I yelled, stepping out of conceal-
ment.

He broke into a run. I sprinted after him as he
yanked open the door and left the car.

I reached the end of the corridor and tugged
at the door and followed him.

That was when I met the cheerful man again.

He was on the platform between the cars. He
must have been waiting for Richter. He had
heard me yell, had seen Richter running, and he
was ready for me when I burst through the door.

Wielding a sap like the one Richter had used
earlier, Mr. Cheerful slugged me. I caught a
glimpse of his face in the light from the car behind us just before the blow landed.

My knees sagged. The man using the sap knew
how to hit and exactly where the blow should
land to put a victim down for the count. I woke
up huddled on the platform, a conductor shaking
me and asking what had happened.

"A man struck me."

"A would-be thief, perhaps. I saw a man leaning over you as I came through the door. He fled
into the next car. If you can describe him . . ."

"I didn't even see his face," I lied.

Richter and his chum had escaped again, but I
considered myself lucky. If the conductor hadn't
appeared, Mr. Cheerful would probably have left
me in worse shape than unconscious.

I assured the conductor I was in condition to

walk. When I was able to break away from him,
I returned to Eva Schmidt's compartment.

"Who is it?" she called out in reply to my
knock.

I changed my voice and spoke in French.
"Porter, madame."

There was a pause. Then a lock clicked. The
door opened a crack. I jammed my foot in the
opening and stuck the Luger into Eva's surprised
face.

"How about that deal we had?" I said in a
rough voice.

"I contacted Horst. But I haven't had time to
get back in touch with you."

Shoving the door shut, I said, "You're lying—
you set the Russian on me."

The woman avoided my eyes. "If he caused
you trouble, it was his idea. I only told him that
you were in on the bidding for the device."

"Beautiful. When you told him that, you
knew damn well what he'd do."

"You can't expect me to worry about your
safety. Not after the way you roughed me up."

I held onto my temper. "What is your connection with Hans Richter?"

Her gaze whipped back to me. "Hans Richter
and I have no connection."

"I saw him leave your compartment. He had a
gunshot wound and he came to you for help.
You bandaged his arm."

Her gaze didn't waver. "I admit that it's true.

But we still have no connection, except that I know West German agents are looking for him. I don't consider that my business. Let them capture their own ex-Nazis."

"Why should he come to you?"

"A few years ago, we knew each other well. I recognized him when I saw him again. I made the mistake of giving him my compartment number, never dreaming he'd get into trouble aboard the train." She smiled slightly. "Now, don't tell me you don't know what I mean when I say I used to know him well."

"Let me tell you about a thought that has just occurred to me, Eva. Maybe Hans Richter is the boss of Topcon. Maybe he's the man you call Horst Blücher."

"Horst does not run around getting shot. He is much too clever for that."

"Then where is he and why doesn't he show himself?" I asked. "What is his reply to my request for a meeting?"

She slid an American cigarette out of a package and lighted it. "Horst says he will consider you a legitimate bidder for the device. But he will only deal with you on this train, and the deal must be made before we reach Sofia. You will make your offer through me."

"Like hell I will," I said. "I'm ready to make my offer for the monitor. But I'm making it only to the boss of Topcon."

She sighed heavily. "He will not like this, but

I will deliver the message. I'll set up the meeting and bring word to your compartment."

"When can I expect to hear from you?"

"After our stop at Belgrade in the morning. I can't make contact with Horst tonight."

"All right," I said. "But this time the meeting better come off. I'm getting very impatient."

In the darkness of my compartment, I stretched out on the bed and listened to the sound of the wheels as the train sped toward Belgrade and the big moment for me and for Ursula.

Ursula hoped to land her fish in Belgrade and I hoped to meet mine. Despite the story Eva Schmidt had given me, I still wondered if the man I was after and Ursula's elusive quarry were one and the same . . .

Because of all the night's excitement and my extreme fatigue, I slept longer than I had expected. A knock on my compartment door awakened me. It was Ursula. The day was bright outside, and we were nearing Belgrade.

"I wanted to say goodbye in case we don't see each other again," she said to me softly.

She hardly looked like an agent. Her tousled blonde hair gave her a young schoolgirl look which was very becoming.

"How nice of you," I said.

When I rose from the bunk, she moved over to me and pressed her lips to mine. I could feel her soft body against my chest. In a long moment the kiss was finished, and she was breathing shallowly.

"I meant that I wanted to *really* say goodbye," she said.

I smiled at her. I guess I had taught her to mix business with a little pleasure. "We'll be in Belgrade soon."

"Saying goodbye doesn't take long."

I smiled again and leaned down and touched my lips to hers. "You're very persuasive," I said.

"I hoped to be." She smiled.

She laid her raincoat down and pulled her boots off as I watched. Then she was pulling her sweater over her head. This time she was not wearing a bra. She looked quite delicious in the morning sun. As she began to take the skirt off, I began unbuttoning my shirt.

In a few minutes we were lying on the bunk together. Her warm nakedness was pressing against me, and I could feel all those curves waiting for my touch.

I was moving my hand slowly along the velvet of her thigh. We had not bothered to pull the shade at the window, and the sun light on her skin made it look peach-colored as she moved her hips against me. I moved my hand up between her legs.

Her breasts were thrusting up toward me, responding to my touch. She had found me and was caressing me slowly and tenderly in a gentle rhythm. Her mouth sought mine hungrily, seeking and nibbling and pressing.

Then I could feel a gentle trembling inside her, and I knew I could not wait. I moved carefully onto her, and we united. A lovely moan came from the depths of her throat.

I did not answer her. I was obsessed with the urgent necessity of finding satisfaction in her. We moved together more and more insistently, and the lovely sounds from her throat seemed to be all around me. Her hips now imprisoned me in sensual desire. The rhythm built and became more violent. There was a cauldron boiling inside me that was ready to overflow. As the sounds from her became one with the distant whistle from the train, the cauldron bubbled over, and she received that hot spilling into her innermost and most secret places.

"A nice way to start a day," I said as I lay beside her. "And we're not saying goodbye. Not just yet. I'll meet the police with you."

"Forget it, Nick," she smiled. "You have your own assignment to think about."

"My assignment just may be related to yours," I replied. "I can't explain now. But we'd better get dressed. We're almost at Belgrade."

We dressed quickly as the train passed through the outskirts of Belgrade. Later, as we walked toward the day coaches, I had an unpleasant thought. If Horst Blücher were in fact Hans Richter and if Ursula managed to arrest him before I found out where the stolen monitor was, or if the monitor was taken into custody along with Richter, my chances of recovering it were slim. The Yugoslavs would certainly not surrender the device to me or to the U.S. government.

In a way, Ursula and I were adversaries for the moment because our missions and immediate goals were contradictory. I was sure that although I had saved Ursula's life, she would not consider postponing her arrest of Richter at Belgrade just because I wanted to recover a piece of electronic hardware from him before he was taken into custody. She would consider her assignment of prime importance because of the enormity of his earlier crimes.

However, the double identity was yet unproven. I saw no way to divert Ursula from her purpose without divulging my mission, and I did not want to do that. So I decided to stick with Ursula during her attempted arrest, watching for Eva Schmidt, and see what would develop in my favor.

We passed through the day coaches slowly, but there was no sign of either Schmidt or Richter. By the time the train moved along the long gray platform of the Belgrade station, we were standing on a platform near the engine. There were a lot of people waiting for the train, and we both realized that Richter could lose himself very easily in such a crowd.

The train finally stopped. I turned to Ursula and gave her a smile. "Well, let's see if we can find your plainclothsmen," I said.

We stepped off the train onto the platform before most of the other passengers and walked toward the busy station building. Ursula was looking for the policemen, and I was watching the train platforms.

"I see them," she said. "Keep an eye out for Richter while I bring the officers. If necessary, we'll have the train searched from front to rear."

Ursula darted away and then I spotted Eva Schmidt. She was alone and in a hurry, pushing her way against the flow of the crowd, headed toward the rear of the train. I forged after Eva, colliding with travelers in my haste.

I saw Hans Richter and his companion, the stocky man with the jovial face, get off the last car. Richter was carrying a piece of luggage and the familiar radio.

They met a cart loaded with luggage and disappeared behind it. I approached them with the luggage hiding me from their view and got close enough to hear their voices.

"You were wise in stalling Carter. This will soon be over." That was Richter. "I will meet the Russian here and close the deal."

"You have the device?" That was Eva.

Richter laughed. "Right here in my radio, where it's been all the time."

I plucked Wilhelmina from inside my jacket.

No wonder Richter had never parted with a radio he didn't play. The satellite monitor was inside the radio's case. Even if it were taken apart, the device would look like part of the circuitry to anyone other than an expert.

Stepping around the end of the luggage cart, I said, "Thanks for arranging the meeting, Eva."

Richter cursed.

"I'll take the radio, Horst. I assume you prefer that name since you're using it now. After I have the radio in my hands, we'll walk over and talk to some policemen who'd like to get to know you, too."

His friends stuck with him to the bitter end. Eva swung her purse and hit my gunhand and Mr. Cheerful jumped me.

I shot the stocky man as we fell. I was in too much of a hurry to wrestle with him.

He was gasping as I threw his weight off me and got to my feet again. He didn't look surprised that I'd pulled the trigger of the Luger. He had expected it when he sprang for me, I thought. He was just trying to give Richter time to make a break.

The ex-Nazi had taken advantage of the opportunity. He was running hard for the door of the station, knocking people aside as he went.

Eva Schmidt ran, too. When she saw that I'd put a bullet in the man who'd jumped me, she turned and lost herself in the crowd. She was heading in the direction of the train, I noticed, but I didn't really care what happened to her.

I raced after Hans Richter.

When he got to the doorway of the big station, he turned. Now he held a Mauser Parabellum in one hand and the radio in his other. He aimed the automatic at my head and fired. The shot resounded along the platform, narrowly missing my left temple. A couple of women screamed. A tall elderly man behind me slumped to the ground—the slug had hit him in his shoulder. There were more screams. As Richter turned and ran into the station, I pulled my Luger, aimed, and fired. Just then he changed his course, and I missed him.

There was no time to see where Ursula and the policemen were. I ran into the station after Richter. There were hundreds of people inside and Richter was cunningly moving among them toward the far doorways that led to the street. I jammed Wilhelmina into my pocket and increased my speed. People were standing and staring, and some were trying to get out of our way. Richter knocked a woman down and kept going. I was gaining, though, and before he managed to reach the doors, I caught him with a shoestring tackle.

Richter hit the floor hard, but he did not lose either the gun or the radio. He turned to blow my head off, but I caught his gunhand and pushed it away. The Mauser roared in the big room, and the slug smashed into the high ceiling. There was more screaming and yelling, and a stampede to get away from the action.

We rolled over twice, each trying for control. Our arms were straining for possession of the gun. It fired again, and a window in a front door shattered. I punched a savage fist into Richter's square face, and his grip weakened on the gun. It fell from his grasp with a quick twist of my arm.

Richter swore, swung his balled-up fist viciously at my head, and connected. I felt the crunching impact beside my ear and I fell backward to the floor. In that instant, Richter was up and reaching for the Mauser.

He retrieved the gun before I could get to him, and when he turned back to me, there was a slight grin on his face. I flicked Hugo down into my palm as he leveled the Mauser at my head. But neither the gun nor the stiletto struck.

"Halten sie! Genug!" It was Ursula.

Richter turned from me and saw Ursula, very grim, pointing the Webley at his back. She was flanked on either side by the two Yugoslav secret policemen in plain clothes. Each man held a stubby revolver aimed at Richter.

"Please put the gun down," the one on Ursula's right ordered.

Richter grunted, dropped the Mauser, and glanced back at me. "Damn you," he said quietly in English.

I walked over to him and yanked the radio

from his hand. The Yugoslavs nodded to me and grabbed his arms.

"We will take him to the customs room for a brief interrogation before moving him to head-quarters," the Yugoslav who had spoken before said to Ursula.

I wanted to get that radio out of there. "I must go to the train for a bag," I said. "I'll be right back."

The same Yugoslav turned to me. "No, please. The train will be held. Come with us first."

He did not seem amenable to argument. "All right," I said as I followed them reluctantly into the room.

It was a rather small room with only a desk and three straight chairs. There was only one window that opened onto the street. It looked stark.

As we stepped into the room, Ursula spoke to the Yugoslav who had insisted I accompany them.

"Oh, his bag!" she exclaimed. "It is on the platform. I will get it."

"Very well," the policeman agreed.

Ursula had just disappeared and closed the door behind her when Richter went into action again. The policemen were still holding his arms. The one who had not yet spoken had taken the radio from me, much to my regret, and had placed it on the desk before us. He was now reaching under his jacket for a pair of handcuffs, but Richter suddenly and quite violently broke free from the other Yugoslav, and sent an elbow into his face. The policeman stumbled backwards and fell heavily to the floor while Richter shoved the other one into me. The man stumbled against me, and I had to catch him to keep him from hitting the floor.

Richter was slugging the first officer and reaching for his gun. I went for Wilhelmina while the man who had hit me tried to regain his balance. Then Richter emerged with the snub-nosed revolver, whirled, and fired at me. I dived for the side of the desk, and he missed.

The policeman who had fallen against me now was going for his gun. Richter fired a shot at him and hit him full in the chest. The man was picked up off his feet and shoved backwards from the sudden impact. His eyes reflected the surprise of sudden death as he crashed against a wall and then slid to the floor.

Richter moved quickly around the desk, grabbing the radio on the way, and made a run for the window. I fired quickly from my cover and grazed his shoulder. He whirled and returned fire. Then he saw the other policeman start for him. He fired again, hitting this one in the abdomen, and the policeman fell heavily on the desk top. Richter then turned and dove through the window, shattering the glass in a fusillade of shards. I fired once more after him as he disappeared, but I did not hit him.

Just then Ursula came through the door.

"He broke away from us," I said. "Come on."
I rushed out the door past curious onlookers and
headed across the station to the front doorways.
Ursula was right behind me.

When I reached the end of the building, I saw
that Richter was gone. I saw a black car, moving
quickly away from the area, a block down the
street, but there was no way of knowing whether
it was Richter.

"The next time I see Mr. Richter," Ursula
said grimly, "I'm going to put a bullet in his
head and ask questions later."

At that moment, the only thing I could think
of was the radio that Richter had grabbed as he
had escaped. I'd had the monitor in my possession momentarily, but now it was lost to me
again. Maybe for good.

Then I remembered Eva.

Nine

"We're after the same man," I said to Ursula.

She looked at me quizzically as I hurried with her back to the station entrance. "What do you mean, Nick?"

"There isn't much time to explain now. Richter is involved in big-time theft, and he has stolen something very valuable to my government in order to sell it to the Communists. That's why he was on the Orient Express."

I could hear the sound of European police sirens as we rushed through the station. There was a crowd around the room where the police had tried to detain Richter. Outside, the Orient Express was getting ready to pull out.

"I'm going to leave you here, Ursula. Tell the police nothing of my involvement if you can avoid it. Check in at the Majestic Hotel at Obilicev Venac 28, and I'll meet you there later. Meanwhile, check the hotels and try to locate Richter. If you do find him, don't try to take him, wait for me."

"When will I see you again?" she asked. "Where are you going now, Nick?"

"There's somebody on that train who might be able to tell us where to find Richter," I said. "So I'm going back aboard. I hope to get back to you later today or early tomorrow."

She smiled. "I am glad our work will keep us together for a while," she said. "Good luck until I see you."

"Same to you," I said.

I reached the platform just as the train was pulling away, and hopped aboard. Blonde and lovely Ursula waved from the doorway, and then she turned to greet the uniformed Yugoslav police.

In just moments the train had cleared the station, and was gliding back out into the Yugoslav countryside. While in Belgrade, the train had taken on a dining car, which was now the last car on the train, behind the sleepers. That made one more place where I would have to look for Eva Schmidt, and it was where I found her. She had just ordered breakfast when I approached her table.

"I ought to put a bullet in you right here," I said. "But I'm going to give you one last chance. Get up and go to your compartment. I'll be right behind you. And no tricks this time. You try something like the last time, and I'll kill you without further discussion."

She hesitated a moment. Then she rose and walked down the aisle of the dining car. I dropped a few bills onto her table for the waiter and followed. Soon we stood before the door of her compartment in Voiture 5.

"In," I ordered.

She unlocked the door. We entered, and I locked it behind us. "Now, what would you like to know?" she asked acidly.

"How to find your lover."

She smiled a hard smile, and ran a hand through her dark hair. "That might be very difficult now. Hans will conclude his sale very shortly, and then he will be a very wealthy man. He will change his identity again and continue to elude the fools who harass him." She laughed. "And we can thank your government for all of it."

I did not like to be laughed at, nor to be called a fool. "You have a way of pressing your luck," I told her. "Where is Richter staying in Belgrade?"

Eva put a smile on her face. She began to disrobe while I spoke to her. I didn't know what she expected to accomplish, but she was soon down to her pants and bra. She had a ripe, full figure.

"If I give you that information, I would take the challenge from your job," she told me.

She locked her eyes on mine as she removed the bra and exposed her breasts.

"You can also be nice and tell me where Topcon headquarters is located," I said to her, watching her now as she slid the black lace panties down over white hips. She was trying to distract me with sex, and she was a lot of woman.

"Maybe we can make some kind of compromise," she purred at me, standing there completely nude. She moved over to me and touched me with her breasts.

"What kind of compromise?" I asked.

She moved her body slightly against me. "You will settle for less than all the information you want, and I will give you a little present instead." She moved her tongue slowly across her lips.

"I can take the present anyway," I reminded her, feeling her hips move against me.

"Yes. But it would not be the same, would it? Not the same at all."

I let the corner of my mouth move. She was good. She and Richter made a smooth team. He had probably used her on other Topcon missions. "And if I were willing to compromise, just what information would you give me?"

She moved the hips more insistently, and it was damned distracting. "I cannot tell you where Topcon headquarters is because I do not know. Richter does not take me there. But I will tell you that he is checking into the Excelsior Hotel in Belgrade at Kneza Milosa 5. I will tell you because he will not be there long, and you will probably not get there in time to find him anyway."

Her hips insinuated themselves closer to me. I put my hand around them and felt the soft flesh move under my touch. I grabbed her chin with the other hand, pulled her to me, planted a savage kiss on her lips. She stood there saucer-eyed and breathless. Then a look of confusion and frustration came into her eyes. She had been in control a moment ago, she had been guiding the action, but suddenly she had lost that control.

I did not release my hold on her chin. I grabbed it in a tighter grip. "You're lying, honey," I insisted.

The confusion changed to apprehension. "No—"

"Oh, yes. I can see it in your eyes." I released her chin, but still held her to me with the other hand. Then I reached into my jacket and drew out Wilhelmina. I stuck the muzzle up against her left breast and sunk it into that soft flesh.

"This isn't like before," I told her. "This time I've run out of patience. Now you listen carefully. I'm going to find out where Richter is hiding out in Belgrade whether you tell me or not. Do you really want to die just to make it a little tougher for me?"

The fear she had shown before had returned to her eyes now. I could tell she was thinking about what I had said. She glanced down at the pistol pressed against her bosom, and then she looked into my eyes.

"The Sava Hotel," she said quietly.

I watched her face, and I was convinced. The

Sava Hotel was the kind of place Richter would pick—small and out-of-the-way.

"And Topcon headquarters is in Lausanne, isn't it?"

She looked quickly at me and then away. I pushed the muzzle of the automatic harder against her breast. She gasped.

"Yes," she answered quickly. "But I honestly don't know the address."

I took the gun away and replaced it in its holster. "I believe you," I said. "And now I must leave you and get off at the next station."

She had not moved away from me. "You do not wish to accept the other part of the arrangement I offered you?"

I ran my hands over the full hips and kissed her mouth. She seemed hungry for me. But I had other things on my mind. I turned and pulled her scarf off a wall hook.

"I'd enjoy it, I know," I admitted. "But I must put business before pleasure, at least sometimes."

I brought the scarf up to her face, and she looked at it questioningly. Then I pulled it across her mouth and tied it at the back. She was suddenly squirming and hitting and making muffled sounds through the scarf. I grabbed her naked body, picked her up, carried her to the bunk and threw her on it. I thought I saw an expectant look come into her eyes for a moment, but I tied her to the bunk with her own belts

and clothing. In a moment, she was spread-ea-
gled on the bunk and glaring at me.

"There won't be much need for a conductor or
porter to beat your door down until you cross
the border into Bulgaria," I told her. "And
that's not until late today. By then, I'll have
reached the Sava Hotel."

Her eyes flared hatred at me, and she mum-
bled something in German through the scarf.

"Don't feel too badly about being tied up," I
smiled at her. "Just try to think of my alternative."

I left her tied nude to the bunk and locked
the compartment door after me. Then I went to
Voiture 7 and my compartment to retrieve my
small piece of luggage. I was ready to get off at
the next whistle stop which came soon after.

Now, I had to get back to Belgrade in the
hope that Richter had gone to the Sava Hotel
despite his being wanted by the Yugoslav police.
I had to find out if he still had the radio in his
possession.

Ten

It was about noon by the time I returned to Central Station in Belgrade on a second class milk train. I took a taxi along Sarajevoska street over to Kneza Mihajla Boulevard, passed the imposing National Museum, made a couple of turns to be sure we were not being followed, and then went directly to the Majestic Hotel on Obilicev Venac. Ursula was very relieved to see me.

"Oh, Nick!" she said, throwing those soft arms around my neck when I entered her room. "I've been pacing the floor. Where the hell have you been."

"I had to take care of some unfinished business. You didn't think I would leave you alone in this wicked Communist capital, did you?" I grinned.

She closed the door behind me. I noticed that she had checked into a very elegant room at a modest rate and that she had a fine view of the street. But now her thoughts were only of Hans Richter.

"Did you find out anything?" she asked.

I lit a cigarette and offered her one, but she declined. I regarded her seriously now. She was pretty tense. "I think I know where Richter is hiding out," I told her. "Unless he panicked and fled the city."

"Is it near here?"

I took a long drag on the cigarette and held it for a moment. "Yes, it's not far from here."

"Where? A hotel?"

I studied Ursula's face for a moment before I spoke. This seemed the appropriate time to tell her about the monitor. I either had to mention it to her or leave her out of the affair completely, and the latter alternative did not seem fair.

"A hotel, yes," I said slowly.

"Which one?" She moved to a telephone on a night table. "I will call the police and have them meet us there."

I shook my head. "No, Ursula."

She looked at me with mild surprise in her lovely blue eyes. Then she put the phone back down. "Why not?"

"Ursula," I began, "I'm going to level with you. Richter has stolen an electronic device from the British government, a U.S. device that is important to the security of the West. He has this device with him. At least, he had it when he left Central Station through the window."

She thought back a moment. "The radio?" she asked.

"Yes, the radio. I'm pretty sure the device is hidden inside it."

"That is why he carried the radio around with him on the train."

I smiled. "That's what I believe at the moment. Now, the Yugoslav police would be happy to extradite him to West Germany to stand trial for war crimes. The Communists are always happy to see a man from the Third Reich caught. But I think you can understand that they might look differently on the matter of returning the electronic device to me."

"I understand Nick," she said.

"I tried to separate Richter from his radio at the station, but I was not successful," I continued. "If I had been, my assignment would have been finished. Now, I still have that radio to recover."

"But, Nick, I can't arrest Richter without the police," she told me. "There is a lot of red tape involved in getting him turned over to the custody of our government. The police must be involved."

"I understand," I said. "But remember that West Germany is one of the free countries that will suffer if this device reaches the hands of KGB. As a matter of fact, I believe that Richter expects to conclude a sale of the device with a Russian right here in Belgrade. They may have done so already. At any rate, Ursula, I'm asking you to give me a crack at Richter and his radio before we call in the Yugoslavs for help in his arrest."

She thought a moment. "I want to help you capture Richter."

"Yes, you may come along," I agreed.

She smiled. "All right, Nick. I will wait before I call the police, but they may have ideas of their own, of course. I think I saw a man watching this hotel. I must assume that they can't quite trust me."

"That makes sense," I said. "You are not, after all, a good Communist."

She smiled that broad German smile, at me, and the blue eyes flashed. "I am not even a good girl," she said.

"I'd have to disagree with that."

She was wearing a robe that tied at the waist, because she had just come from the shower. She untied the robe now and let it fall open—she was nude underneath. "I suppose I had better get dressed," she said.

I looked at her curves hungrily. "I suppose."

The robe dropped to the floor. I let my eyes travel over the thrusting breasts, and small waist, and the sweep of milky hips and thighs. I remembered Eva on the train, and I knew that Eva had triggered something inside me that was now being caressed and nurtured by the sight of Ursula.

"On the other hand," she said, moving to close the distance between us, "if Richter is at that hotel now, he will probably be there just a little longer."

"Probably," I said.

She began nibbling at my ear. And I let her start undressing me.

Ursula was building a fire in me that promised to rage out of control very soon. I helped her take the rest of my clothing off, and then I took her to the big double bed across the room. We lay down together, and the next thing I knew, she was moving over on me in the male position.

Her breasts hung down over my chest in lovely pendulous arcs. She let herself down closer to me, and the tips of her breasts rubbed gently across my chest as she kissed my face and neck with her moist lips.

She moved down to my abdomen, planting kisses delicately, and the fire burned in my groin. Then she moved further down, caressing with the full warm lips, until I could stand it no longer.

"Now, *liebling?*" she asked.

"Now," I answered huskily.

I pushed her over on the bed and straddled her, breathless, eager. The milky thighs came up and surrounded me, and I remember feeling them lock securely behind me as we made union. The fire erupted into a volcanic holocaust. Then there were sweet smells and lovely sounds and hot flesh as we reached a climax.

When I got a look at the Sava Hotel, I realized why Richter had chosen it. It would best be described as a flea-trap in the States—an old, decrepit building that looked as if it should have been pulled down long ago in the old section of town. The sign outside the place was so weatherbeaten that one could pass it without realizing it was a hotel. It looked like the kind of place where the management would look the other way for questionable guests.

The hotel had only twenty rooms, and I could see from the number of keys placed in the mail boxes behind the desk that only a half dozen were taken. I was not surprised when the sleazy Yugoslav desk clerk did not ask to see our passports, but merely took their numbers. He considered it only a formality to satisfy the police.

While the clerk came around the desk to take my one piece of luggage, I glanced at the mail boxes again and memorized those that revealed occupancy of particular rooms. Then we climbed the stairs with the clerk. When he had opened the door and had put down my luggage, I tipped him.

Just as the clerk was leaving, a door down the hall opened, and Hans Richter came out into the corridor. I shoved Ursula back from the doorway and hid from sight myself. A moment later I sneaked a look and saw Richter and two men standing in the corridor with their backs to me. They were preparing to leave another man, whose room they had just left. The other man was Ivan Lubyanka.

Apparently Richter had sent Lubyanka to this place when he had left the Orient Express at Pivka. Now, even though Richter appeared to have found a different hiding place because of the incident at the station, he had come here with these men, who were obviously Topcon agents, to discuss the sale of the monitor device with the Russian.

Richter was not carrying the radio. Maybe he did not trust the KGB. He and his cohorts walked down the corridor to the stairway as Lubyanka closed his door.

I turned to Ursula. "It's Richter and his friends," I said. "Follow them and see where they go. Try not to get yourself killed. In the meantime, I'm going to pay a visit to a Russian friend of mine down the hall. I'll meet you at the Majestic at three. Wait an hour after that, and if I don't show, you're on your own."

She looked into my face for a brief, tender moment. "All right, Nick."

I smiled. "See you later."

"Yes."

Ursula disappeared down the corridor after Richter and his men.

A few minutes later, I knocked on the door of Lubyanka's room. After a short pause, Lubyanka's voice came from the other side of the door. "Yes?"

I was pretty good at dialects and voices, especially after I had had a chance to hear them, so I cleared my throat and tried my best to sound like Hans Richter.

"Blücher," I said.

The lock on the door clicked as I pulled out the Luger. When the door opened and I saw Lubyanka's surprised face, I did not wait for an invitation to enter the room. I kicked at the door savagely and smashed it into the room. It hit Lubyanka in the chest and head and knocked him to the floor.

Lubyanka started for his gun on a distant table, but I stopped him. "Hold it right there."

He turned and saw the Luger aimed at his head. Then glanced at the distance between him and the Webley and decided it was a lousy risk.

"It is you again," he said bitterly.

"I'm afraid so, old man. All right, on your feet. And keep away from your plaything on the table."

Lubyanka rose slowly, blood dripping from his cheek and mouth. His lip was already swelling. I moved to the door and closed it, keeping an eye on the KGB man every moment. His eyes held a great dislike for me.

"Now," I said, "you and I are going to have a nice talk."

"We have nothing to talk about," he answered grimly.

"I think we do."

He grunted and moved his hand to the cut on

his cheek. "You have come to the wrong man, I'm afraid."

"Maybe," I said. "But if I have, it will be too bad for you." I watched his face as the impact of that statement sunk in.

"We haven't made a deal yet," he told me. "Consequently, I do not have what you are looking for."

"If Richter still has it, where does he keep it?" I asked.

"Richter?"

"Excuse the lapse. He's Horst Blücher, to you."

Lubyanka thought about that a moment. "I do not have any idea where the device is. He is very secretive and evasive."

"Maybe he doesn't trust you, Lubyanka," I said, needling him a little.

He gave me a look. "I do not trust him."

The corner of my mouth moved. It always gave me a little pleasure to see two unpleasant people trying to outsmart each other. "Well, there is one thing for sure, Lubyanka. You know where to contact him. And I want you to tell me that."

Lubyanka had moved over to an unmade bed. I watched him closely and kept the Luger trained on him. "He has not told me where he is staying," he said slowly.

"You're lying, Lubyanka. And that will get you a 9mm slug in the head." I moved closer to him. "I want the truth, and I want it now. Where can I find Richter?"

Lubyanka's eyes suddenly looked flat, desperate. Surprising me, he grabbed a big pillow from the bed and turned toward me with it in front of him. I had no idea what he was doing, so I took no chances. I fired, and the Luger exploded in the small room.

The slug was buried in the thick pillow and never reached to Lubyanka's chest. In the meantime, Lubyanka hurled himself at me, still holding the pillow between us. I raised the level of my aim and fired again at his head, but my shot narrowly missed as he fell on me.

Lubyanka hit at my gun arm and knocked it high, but I still held the gun. Now the pillow was gone, and Lubyanka was twisting violently at my arm with both hands. We hit against a wall, and I lost the gun.

Then we both slid to the floor, struggling for dominance. I threw a fist into Lubyanka's already bloody face, and he managed to return the blow before breaking away from me. Then he was reaching for the Webley that was now near him on the table.

He grabbed the gun before I could reach him, but he could not get at the trigger assembly in time to fire it. When I reached him, he hit out savagely with the gun, striking me across the side of the head with the heavy barrel.

I fell back near a window, against the wall.

Lubyanka then got to his feet and pointed the Webley at me again, but I found the strength to grab at his gun hand and pull him before he could fire. He sailed past me and crashed through the window. The glass shattered loudly and rained down around me as I turned and watched Lubyanka's body hurtle into the open air outside—his arms were spread wide, as he grasped for something to save him.

There was a short silence as Lubyanka fell, then I heard a scream. I leaned out through the broken glass and saw that he had hit a second floor balcony. He was impaled on the pickets of an iron balustrade, facing up with his eyes still open, and two of the pickets protruded through his chest and abdomen.

I swore at myself. Lubyanka would tell me nothing now. Retrieving Wilhelmina, I quickly left the small room and hurried down the corridor just as the sound of footsteps came from the front stairs. I avoided them by using the rear service stairs to reach the street.

Eleven

"This is the place. This is where Richter went with the two men," Ursula told me.

We were huddled in a dark doorway on a narrow street, staring through the night at an old building across the way. Ursula was becoming very anxious, but she tried not to show it.

"Do you think they might have seen you following them?" I asked.

"I don't think so," she said.

The building across the street was an apartment house. Ursula had told me that they had entered the street room on the second floor, but there were no lights on at the moment.

"Well, let's go up there and take a look," I suggested.

"All right, Nick." She reached into her purse for the Webley.

"I want you to keep me well covered up there," I said. "This could be a trap."

"You can count on me, Nick."

When we got up to the room where we supposed Richter and his men had been, it appeared to be vacant. I entered carefully, Wilhelmina out, but no one was there.

"Come on in," I told Ursula.

She joined me, closed the door, and glanced around the place. It was a large room with a private bath. Paint was flaking off the walls, and the plumbing looked antique. There was a lumpy cot in a corner, a scarred wooden table, and several straight chairs to one side.

"Some place," I commented. I slipped the Luger back into its holster. I walked over to the cot. It seemed that somebody had recently lain on it.

"There is no luggage or anything here," Ursula noted. "We may have lost him already."

"Let's take a look around," I said.

We tore the place apart. There was evidence that Richter had been there—a butt of one of his favorite cigarettes; a bottle of wine, almost empty; and in a wastebasket, his discarded train ticket. I could find nothing that indicated he would be returning to this room. In fact, all the evidence indicated that he had left it for good.

"Now what do we do?" Ursula asked.

"I don't know," I told her. I wandered back into the bathroom and glanced slowly around. It seemed to me that there was some place in the room that we had overlooked. I looked into the empty medicine chest again.

Then I turned to the toilet. The top was down on it. I lifted the lid and looked into the bowl.

There I saw the piece of wet, crumpled paper floating in the clear water.

I fished it out and took a look at it. It was only a fragment of paper from a larger piece that had evidently been torn up and flushed to oblivion, but there were several handwritten letters on it.

"I've got something," I said.

Ursula came and looked over my shoulder. "What is it?"

"It looks as if Richter tried to get rid of this down the toilet. Can you make out what the letters are?"

She took a look at it. "This is Richter's handwriting," she said. She made a face as she turned the note slightly. It looks like it is written in Serbo-Croatian, Nick. Perhaps the beginning of the word *national*. And another letter, the start of another word."

I squinted at it. "National. But what's the second word?"

"M—U—S—museum, The National Museum."

I looked quickly at her. "The museum. Does it have a checkroom?"

"I suppose so," she said.

"Richter would have no reason to use the museum for a rendezvous," I said. "We know he has already met Lubyanka at the Sava Hotel, and possibly here."

"That is true," Ursula said, but not following me.

"Well, let's say you wanted to deposit that radio somewhere for safekeeping for a couple of days. You can't use a baggage checkroom at the Central Station or the airport because the police are watching for you there. But why not use the checkroom at a public place like the museum?"

"But articles are checked there only for the time the visitor is in the museum," Ursula reminded me.

I thought about that a moment. "They would keep an article for a couple of days, though, expecting its owner to return. But let's say Richter did not want to depend on that possibility. Maybe he checked the radio at the museum and then called them later in the day to say that he had neglected to pick it up when he left. He would have promised to get the radio within twenty-four or forty-eight hours. He would be assured then that they would take special care to hold it for him."

"That is a good theory, Nick. It is worth checking out."

"We'll be at the museum first thing in the morning," I said. "If Richter finds out about Lubyanka tonight, he will probably decide to leave Belgrade immediately, but not without that radio. If he did stash it at the museum, we would want to beat him there. It may be our last chance for contact with him."

"In the meantime," she said, "you need some

rest. And I have an especially comfortable room at the Majestic."

"That's a nice offer," I said.

We were at the National Museum when it opened the following morning. It was a sunny spring day in Belgrade. There were bright green buds on the tall trees in Kalamegdan Park. The hydrofoil tour boats plied the placid waters of the Danube, and the bustling traffic seemed somehow less hectic. But the museum itself sat monolithic and gray in the bright morning; it was a vivid reminder that Ursula and I were not there for diversion.

The interior was all high ceilings and sterile glass cases, a striking contrast with the sunny morning on the other side of its thick walls. It didn't take us long to find the checkroom. The Yugoslav on duty there was still waking up.

"Good morning," I greeted him. "A friend of ours left a portable radio here and forgot to take it away with him. He has sent us to pick it up." I was speaking in my best German accent.

He scratched his head. "Radio? What is this?"

I decided to try speaking to him in Serbo-Croatian. "A radio. One that is carried on a strap."

"Ah," he said. He moved to a corner of the small room while I held my breath and reached toward a shelf. He pulled down Richter's radio. "I have one left here by a fellow named Blücher, a Swiss."

"Yes," I said, glancing at Ursula. "That's it. Horst Blücher is the full name."

He looked on a slip. "Yes. Do you have some identification, Mr. Blücher? I don't seem to remember your face."

I controlled my impatience. I had already decided to take the radio by force if it was necessary. "I am not Horst Blücher," I said deliberately. "We are his friends who have come to claim the radio for him."

"Ah. Well, Mr. Blücher should have come himself, you see. That is the rule."

"Yes, of course," I said. "But Mr. Blücher has fallen ill and is unable to come for the radio. We hope you'll understand. You will be doing him a great favor if you give us the radio to take to him."

He looked at me suspiciously and then at Ursula. "Did he give you the claim slip?"

Now Ursula put on an act. "Oh, dear! He mentioned that we should take the slip just before we left. But he forgot to give it to us. He is quite ill." Then she turned on the charm. "I hope you will not be technical about the slip. Mr. Blücher so wanted to hear some beautiful Yugoslav music while he is here."

"Ah," the man said, looking into her cool blue eyes. "Well, I can understand that. Here, you may take the radio. I have no facilities for storing it here anyway."

"Thank you very much," I told him.

He ignored me and handed the radio to Ursula. "Tell your friend to get well soon so that he may enjoy his stay in Belgrade."

"Thank you," Ursula said.

She took the radio, and we left the checkroom. But on our way out of the building, I found that my victory was short-lived. Two men stepped out of an alcove in a corridor, and no one else was around. They both held guns. They were the two Topcon men we had seen earlier with Richter, the men Ursula had followed.

"Stop there, please," the taller one ordered.

I groaned inaudibly. Another few minutes and the monitor device would have been mine. Damn these men! This was the second time I had been in possession of it, only to have it snatched away from me. Ursula was not quite as upset as I was. She had lost all contact with Richter, despite the recovery of the radio, and now these men had reestablished that contact. I found myself wondering if she would live to benefit from this turn of events.

The shorter man, a square fellow with a broken nose, waved his automatic at the radio. "Put the radio on the floor between us along with your purse—" he glanced at me—"and your gun."

"Then step away from them," the taller man ordered.

Ursula looked at me, and I nodded assent. With two guns aimed at us, there was little room for argument. She stepped forward and set the radio and her purse with the Webley in it on the floor. I slowly pulled the Luger from my jacket, watching for any kind of opportunity to use against them, but both guns were now centered on my chest. I placed the Luger on the floor beside the radio and purse. I still had Hugo up my sleeve, but it looked as if there would be little opportunity to use it.

"Very good," the tall Topcon agent said. He had dark hair and a very thin face. He motioned to the other man, who stepped forward, opened Ursula's purse, and removed the Webley. He stuck that and Wilhelmina in his jacket pocket. Then he picked up the radio.

"Now come with us," the tall man said.

Ursula looked at me again. "We'd better do what the man says," I told her.

They got us out of the building without anyone noticing and took us to a gray Fiat sedan outside. Ursula and I were told to get into the rear of the car. The tall man got behind the wheel, and the one with the broken nose got in beside him, but he faced us with the automatic aimed at my chest.

"We will go for a little pleasure ride now," the one with the gun told me with a great deal of satisfaction.

The car entered the stream of morning traffic. I saw that both rear doors were locked with special locks. It seemed there was no way to beat the man with the gun. Richter had apparently decided that it was best to get rid of us so that he could continue his negotiations without interference. I was beginning to understand how he had eluded all kinds of police and government agents for so many years: he was intelligent, efficient, and completely free of conscience.

We were driving out of Belgrade. We went along the Brankova Prizrenska Boulevard until we got to the river, then followed the Kara Dordeva out of town to the south. In a short while, we were in open, rolling country.

"Where are you taking us?" I finally asked.

"You will know very soon," the broken-nosed one said, giving me a harsh grin. His accent was German, while the tall man's was French. It was quite a cosmopolitan outfit, this Topcon.

His prediction was correct. In another fifteen minutes, after winding around a couple of country roads, we came to an isolated country house. The driver pulled to a stop before it and ordered us out.

Ursula and I climbed out of the Fiat. I had no idea where we were; I only knew that we were south of the city. It made sense that Richter would leave Belgrade, since the police were combing the city for him. By now it was impossible for him to travel by public transportation. I wondered whether he knew about Lubyanka yet.

"Into the house," the tall man ordered, waving his revolver at us. Both guns were pointed at us again. I followed orders.

Inside, the house looked even smaller than it had appeared from the exterior. But it was all Richter needed. In a moment, after the tall gunman had called for him, Richter came into the room from the kitchen.

"Well," he said when he saw us, "What a pleasant surprise." He reached for the radio that the tall man had placed on a table. "You almost got it, didn't you?"

"So far you've been just a step ahead of us," I said. "But your luck can't hold out forever, Richter."

I saw the hirelings glance at me when I used his real name. Apparently he was known to them only as Blücher. Richter grinned at me and then moved over and slugged me in the face.

I fell heavily to the floor. Ursula gasped and bent over me. A trickle of blood ran from my mouth. I lay there and looked up at Richter and hated him. That hatred would make me try a little harder if I ever got any chance to move against him.

Ursula looked up at Richter. "Nazi butcher!" she hissed.

Anger flushed Richter's face. He slapped her hard across the face, and she fell down beside me.

Richter turned to the men who had brought us. "Handcuff them there and there." He pointed to a room divider that had a series of thin iron bars built adjacent to the doorway of the kitchen, and to an old iron radiator on a side wall. "So they are separated."

The broken-nosed man cuffed both of Ursula's wrists to the radiator, and the tall man chained me to the outside post of the room divider. My hands were in back of me, with each wrist cuffed and the connecting chain around the bar. I had to stand and Ursula was obliged to sit on the floor, her back against the radiator.

"All right, get it," Richter ordered to the tall gunman.

The tall man disappeared into a small bedroom and returned a moment later with a home-made bomb. There was enough dynamite attached to it to blow up two houses the size of the one we were in. Richter glanced at me with a grin, took the bomb from the tall man's hands, and set the device on a table in the center of the room, about halfway between Ursula and me.

"André is very good with these things," Richter remarked as he set the clock that was the trigger for the bomb. "A bullet would be neater, of course, but this is so much more complete. It is highly unlikely that the authorities will be able to identify your bodies after the explosion and fire. I hope this example will be a warning to any who might come after you."

"I expect it will make them think," I said. I looked carefully at the bomb, which was set and ticking. Richter was right. There would be little left for examination if that thing went off.

"We will never give up until you are in the custody of the people whose name you blemished," Ursula said in a tight voice.

Richter glanced at her. "I blemished?" he said acidly. "It is too bad you were not around when it was all going on, fräulein. The Third Reich did not depend on me alone to accomplish its goals. All of us were Nazis then. When we were defeated, a few weak ones turned on the rest and suddenly became anti-Nazi.

"You're a lying dog," Ursula hissed.

"Now it is fashionable to befriend former enemies and run about with socialists and betray old ideals," he continued slowly.

"And Nazis end up working with Communists," I reminded him.

He turned hard eyes on me. "That is business, pure and simple. It is what a man has to do when he is hunted like a dog by those who turned on him."

"Killing us will not save you, Herr Richter!" Ursula said loudly. "You will be apprehended, and you will pay for what you have done."

He gave her a bitter grin. "You now have less than twenty minutes to convince yourself of that." Without waiting for an answer, he turned to his henchmen. "Disable the Lamborghini. We will take the Fiat down to the Dragoman Pass station at Crveni Krst. It should be safe to get aboard the train there."

"Yes, Herr Blücher," the tall man said. The two turned and went outside.

As the gunmen tampered with the Lamborghini outside, Richter turned once more to me, "You have temporarily aborted my deal with the Russians. But only temporarily. For that you will now pay with your lives."

So he knew about Lubyanka.

"When I leave here, I will not only have all the time I want in Sofia to resume negotiations for the sale of the satellite monitor, but I will have the Bonn government off my neck for quite some time. You see, everything works out very well for me, as usual." He walked to the door. Outside, the Fiat engine was started. "*Auf wiedersehen.* Or perhaps I should just say, goodbye?"

He turned and was gone. In a moment the Fiat pulled away, and the sound gradually diminished as they drove back to the main road.

Ursula and I looked at the ticking bomb simultaneously and then at each other. Ursula was biting her lower lip and shaking her head. "I should have killed Richter the moment I recognized him."

"Cool it," I said. "We have less than fifteen minutes left now. That doesn't leave much time for deep thinking."

"I can't move," Ursula said, rattling her handcuffs against the radiator.

"Try to relax," I told her, calmly. "Your anx-

iety can be contagious, and I have to work something out here."

The damned ticking of the bomb on the table
was like our heartbeats ticking out their last. I
tuned it out and twisted to look at the bars behind me. I pulled on the one I was attached to,
and it bent and then sprung back. I frowned and
scraped the chain of the handcuffs against the
bar. It made a soft sound, not the sharp, grating
one that metal makes. The bars were not metal
after all, but wood painted to look like black iron.
Then I remembered Hugo. They had not found
Hugo, my stiletto.

Hope sprung into my chest and caused my gut
to tighten even more. I moved my right arm,
but nothing happened. I was greatly handicapped
in my movements. I moved around facing Ursula
and leaned away from the slim wooden bar.

"What are you doing, Nick?"

"Trying to save our lives," I said curtly. I had
no time for chatter.

I moved my arm again, and Hugo slipped
down into my palm. I worked the knife into
position so that my grip was firm on the handle.
Twisting my wrist sharply, I managed to apply
the sharp edge of Hugo's blade to the wood of
the bar just under my hands. I cut at the bar
and felt the knife blade bite into the wood. The
wood was hard, but Hugo was honed to a fine
edge for cutting. I made small whittling motions

with the blade and could feel a couple of chips fall away.

I glanced over at Ursula. "I'm trying to chop this damned bar down," I explained. I could not see the face of the clock on the bomb. "How much time is there?"

"Just over ten minutes," Ursula said, craning to see the face of the clock.

"Jesus," I said, angry that so much time had elapsed.

I whittled away. I did not care to cut all the way through the bar. I just wanted to weaken it. There were a lot of chips on the floor. I stopped chopping and pulled hard on the bar. There was a tiny crackling noise, but the wood did not break. The cuffs had now cut deeply into my wrists. I whittled some more until I could finally feel a deep gash in the wood. I steeled myself for the pressure of the cuffs against my wrists and looked over at Ursula.

"Time," I said.

"Six minutes."

I braced my feet under me and pulled with all my strength. There was a loud cracking noise as the wooden bar splintered. I plunged headlong onto the floor and almost hit the table where the bomb was resting.

My hands were still cuffed behind me, but I struggled to my feet. I could feel blood on my wrists. I stood beside the table to get a look at the bomb. If I knew Richter, and I thought I was beginning to, he would have the bomb rigged so that any jarring of it such as picking it up would set it off ahead of time. I leaned down to check out the wiring and saw that I was right. I either had to disarm the bomb without moving it or get Ursula free somehow of the radiator.

The bomb was set to go off when the minute hand reached the half hour, and there were only four minutes to go. I didn't have much time.

"We've got to get you off that thing," I said as I turned to Ursula. "I can't move the bomb."

"But how can I get free?" she asked, trying to keep the panic from her voice.

I leaned down and examined how she was shackled to the metal. There was only one way to free her, and that was to pick the lock of the handcuffs. But that operation would require several minutes, even if I had my hands in front of me. I slipped Hugo into a back trousers pocket; I would not need it. Then I examined the radiator carefully.

The pipe from the basement that joined the radiator was all rusted out. It looked as if the radiator had not been in use for years. Also, the plates that anchored the radiator to the wooden floor appeared old and loose.

I stepped back and surveyed the scene from a short distance. The radiator was placed about a foot from the wall. There was enough room for what I had in mind. I positioned myself squarely before the radiator and glanced at Ursula.

"Brace yourself," I said. "I'm going to give this thing a hard kick."

"All right, Nick," she said.

I glanced at the clock. There were two minutes to go. Raising my leg and bending my knee, I kicked out viciously at the radiator with my right foot.

There was a wrenching of metal and wood as I connected, and Ursula was thrown backwards against the radiator. I heard her make a sharp sound in her throat. When I looked to see the results, I found a pile of rust on the floor. The radiator had come off the pipe completely and was leaning back against the wall. The plates that had held it to the floor had been torn loose, but they still had rotten wood attached to them. One of the plates was still clinging to the wooden floor at the anchor, so I kicked out again and freed it completely.

Ursula was bruised and covered with rust.

"I'm afraid you're going to have to lug your end of this thing," I told her. "Get up. Fast."

She struggled to her feet, lifting one end of the radiator with her. It was heavy for her, but her adrenalin was flowing. I moved sidewise, grabbed the other end with my cuffed hands, and hoisted the radiator to thigh level. I looked at the clock on the bomb. There was less than a minute left.

"Move!" I said. "Out the door!"

Ursula stumbled out of the open doorway, still

hooked to the big piece of accordion-shaped metal. I followed her, having to walk almost backwards.

"Walk very fast," I said. "Don't run. We have to make at least fifty yards. To that depression in the ground over there."

She obeyed orders, grunting and sweating. It was awkward as hell. Once Ursula fell to her knees while I almost lost my end of the radiator. "Get up," I said in a calm voice.

She did. The clock in my head told me that we had only about fifteen seconds. We moved quickly to the shallow depression in the field adjacent to the house, and stumbled into it. Just as we fell to the ground, a deafening explosion ripped the calm day behind us.

The shock waves hurt my ears and blew our hair into our faces. Then we were assailed by a welter of dirt and debris. Big, heavy pieces of timber rained down around us. In a moment it was over, and we looked toward the house. A big cloud of smoke curled skyward, and the little that was left of the cottage was in flames.

"My goodness," Ursula exclaimed, evidently imagining what would have happened to her if the radiator had not come loose. Her blonde hair was straggly, and there was dirt on her face.

"We were lucky," I said.

I got Hugo and went to Ursula's end of the radiator to begin picking the lock on her cuffs. It required over ten minutes. When she was finally free, she rubbed her wrists for a long moment and drew a deep breath. Then she set to work with Hugo to remove my cuffs. It took her about the same time, with her hands free. My wrists had been cut by the cuffs, but the blood was already caking over the wounds.

"Now what, Nick?" Ursula asked.

"Now we head for the Dragoman Pass after Richter."

"They have a headstart on us," she said. "And we don't have a car. They took some parts from the Lamborghini."

"I know," I said, glancing toward the Italian car near the house. Some of its glass had been broken, and the paint had been blasted off one side by the explosion. "But Richter made it clear that he is getting back aboard the Orient Express at the Pass. He intends to cross the border into Bulgaria at Dimitrovgrad. So we don't have to concern ourselves with getting to Crveni Krst when Richter gets there, but before the train leaves. It might just be possible, if we get down to the main road and catch a ride right away."

"Then let's start walking," Ursula said.

Twelve

It was quite a hike to the road. Ursula did not complain, but I could tell that the strain of the past twenty-four hours was telling on her. About a half hour after we left the scene of the burning cottage, we reached the only road that passes through that part of the country.

"It looks pretty lonely," Ursula said.

The road stretched out flat along the river valley in either direction for as far as the eye could see, but there were no cars on it. It was so quiet that it was difficult to believe that any traffic would ever come past.

"It makes me want to forget Richter and just enjoy the peace and quiet," I said.

"Yes," Ursula agreed. She went and sat on the grassy bank by the roadside, and I joined her there.

Ursula leaned back in the long grass with her elbows propped under her. She closed her eyes and listened to a bird in a nearby field. It was a soft, sunny spring day with an enervating magic in the balmy air. A clump of poplars, green buds decorating their lacy branches, whispered nearby, and the breeze that moved the trees also gently rippled the long grass in the field that paralleled the road. It was the kind of day and place, and the kind of company, that makes an agent wonder what the hell he is doing in his particular profession.

Ursula's short, dark skirt was hiked up around her upper thighs, and she looked very good lying there. A bedroom is not the only perfect setting for love-making, as I had discovered on other happy occasions. Often I find a perfect place in the most unexpected circumstances. But this opportunity, considering we were hoping for a car any minute, was less than favorable.

"Nick! It's a car!" Ursula pointed.

It was a Citroën sedan, approaching us at high speed.

"Good," I said. "I'll try to stop it." I climbed out on the roadway and waved my arms in a wide arc. The car began to slow down immediately, and in a moment it had pulled over onto the shoulder beside us.

Two young Italian men were inside, and they were headed toward the border themselves.

"Are you going as far as Crveni Krst at the Dragoman Pass?" I asked.

They were both thin young men with long hair. The driver glanced at Ursula and apparently liked what he saw. "We will make a point of going to Crveni Krst," he said in a thick accent. "Please get in."

We did, and the car roared away down the highway. I was glad that they enjoyed driving fast, because our time was short. In fact, we might have already lost our chance to get there in time.

At first the young men made overtures to Ursula. They offered cognac and wanted to stop for a rest. But when they saw that Ursula was not one for group sex, they went back to enjoying the sunny day. We arrived at the mountain village of Crveni Krst, where Richter had undoubtedly headed, by around two P.M. The Italians took us right to the train station, and I hurriedly thanked them for the ride. Then Ursula and I went inside.

It was not a big place, and it had the stark gray look of most stations along that line in Yugoslavia. We looked quickly around the waiting room and saw that neither Richter nor his two henchmen were there. As I glanced out at the station platform, I saw a train moving away.

"Come on," I said to Ursula.

By the time we got out there, the train was already at the end of the platform, picking up speed. It was the Orient Express.

"Damn!" I said.

I looked down to the end of the building to an open area where a couple of cars were parked, and I saw the Fiat that Richter had driven from the country house outside Belgrade.

"Look," I said. "His car. He is aboard that train."

I grabbed Ursula's hand and started pulling her after me as I ran down the platform toward the car.

"What are we doing, Nick?" she asked as we ran.

"We're going to get the Butcher of Belgrade," I told her.

We stopped at the Fiat, and I looked down the track. I had to catch that train. If Richter got into Bulgaria, my chances of getting him and the radio were slim indeed. He would have all the KGB help he needed there.

I jumped into the low sports car and grabbed at some wires under the dashboard. The train was slowly disappearing around a bend in the track. I crossed the wires, and the engine leaped into action.

"Get in and drive!" I yelled at Ursula above the noise of the car.

I moved over to the passenger's seat, and Ursula got in behind the wheel.

I pointed to the place where the Orient Express was disappearing around the curve of track. "Follow that damned train!" I said.

She glanced at me for just a second. Then the car shot out of the parking area and headed along the shoulder of the track.

I looked ahead of us and saw that although the bank was steep on either side of the track near the village, there was room for the narrow sports car if Ursula could steer well enough.

"Switch over to the other side of the track at this crossing up here," I told her as we bumped along with the left wheels on the ties. "I want to be next to the train if we catch it."

She did as I told her, and we bumped along on the left side of the track now. Ursula's eyes were wide as she fought to keep control of the car. The ties under the wheels on the right shook the car considerably, and there were ruts under the other wheels, but Ursula kept the Fiat on the shoulder of the tracks. In just moments the train was in sight again, and we were gaining on it.

"Faster," I urged her.

Ursula pressed the accelerator, and we shot ahead. The train was only yards away. It was gliding along smoothly in comparison to our own wild ride. We hit a bump, and the car swerved to the left. For a moment, I thought we were going over the embankment. But Ursula fought for control, and finally we were moving along well again. The rear platform of the dining car was now within twenty feet. I opened the door of the Fiat and glanced over at Ursula.

"When I get aboard, drive back to town and wait at the station for me. I'll try to take him alive for you if he lets me."

She nodded desperately, her knuckles white over the steering wheel. I took one last look at her and stood up on the step of the open door of the car. We were alongside the rear platform of the train. The open door of the car prevented our getting too close, but I needed another foot.

"Closer!" I yelled back at her.

The car bumped and swerved and moved away from the train. Then we were right up against the train, the open door clanging against the structure of the platform. It was now or never. I jumped across the four feet of rushing ground, grabbed at the railing of the platform, and found it. I pulled myself up on the platform and climbed over the rail. Then I looked back and saw that Ursula was already slowing the car. I gave her a wave, and she blinked the headlights at me as she drove slowly to the next crossing.

I straightened my clothing and brushed my hair back off my forehead. I had gotten aboard without killing myself or Ursula. Now I had to find Hans Richter before we reached the border.

I entered the dining car and scanned the faces of the few people who were there for an afternoon drink. None of them was Richter or his men. I moved through the car casually as if I were just taking a walk along the train. If a conductor stopped me for a ticket, I could purchase one on board—maybe a second class ticket, but I could care less, for I had no expectation of relaxing and enjoying this trip.

I walked through the two sleeping cars slowly, watching for any sign of Richter, but I saw none. I didn't see anything in the day coaches, either. The only faces I saw on the train were those of happy holiday travelers. If Richter were aboard, he was playing it safe and hiding. He had probably managed to procure one or more sleeping compartments for him and his men, and they would be inside them, waiting to cross into Bulgaria at Dimitrovgrad.

There was an advantage I had gained since my experience on the last train, however. I was now sure of Hans Richter's identity, and I knew what he looked like. I could describe him to the train officials.

It took me ten minutes to find a porter, but when I did, he was very cooperative.

"Let me see," he said in Serbo-Croatian, "a man such as you describe did board at Crveni Krst, I believe. Yes, now I remember. I just saw the fellow entering Compartment 8 in the next sleeping car."

In a moment I stood outside the door of Compartment 8. I pulled out Wilhelmina and prepared myself mentally for whatever might come. I told myself that Hans Richter was not going to get away this time; he was not going to leave this train alive. I stepped back from the door a moment, lifted my right foot, and kicked savagely at it.

The door crashed into the compartment and I followed it. The Luger was ready to fire. I stopped just inside the door and scanned the interior. It was empty.

I moved in quickly and closed the door behind me. My guess about Richter's taking two or more compartments was undoubtedly correct. He had probably acquired another compartment under the name of one of the other men, and he was probably there right at this moment, planning his next move to sell the satellite monitor in Sofia.

I looked around. There was no luggage and no radio, but there was a jacket lying on the bunk It was the one that Richter had been wearing earlier.

I could wait for him here, or I could try to find where he and his men were hiding. I turned to the bunk and pulled down the covers to make sure he had not hidden the radio somewhere there. While I was turned away from the door, I heard a click of the handle. I whirled back to face the sound as I reached for the reholstered Luger.

The broken-nosed Topcon agent stood in the door, and his tall companion was right behind him.

The man with the broken nose went for his gun, but I beat him. While his hand was still in his jacket, Wilhelmina's ugly muzzle was already pointing at his surprised face. His tall companion didn't even try.

"Take your hand out of your coat. Carefully," I said.

He did.

"Now both of you, step inside."

I stepped backward two paces, and then edged into the compartment. I ordered the tall man to close the door behind him. When he had done that, I carefully disarmed both men.

"How did you do it?" the broken-nosed one asked. "How did you get out of the cottage?"

"Never mind that," I said, keeping them both together in front of me. "Where is Richter?"

"Ah," the tall man said, grinning. "You have followed the wrong men, my friend. He did not get aboard this train."

He was closest to me. I swung the Luger at the side of his head and connected. He grunted and fell against the compartment wall.

"You want to try again?" I asked.

The tall man was shocked and dazed. The other one spoke for him. "He is aboard," he said. "But we don't know where. We left him at the other end of the train."

"This compartment is for one person," I said. "Did you two take a separate compartment?"

The broken-nosed man hesitated while the tall one looked at him darkly. "Yes."

"What's the number?"

"Don't tell him!" the tall man shouted loudly.

I kicked him in the lower leg, and he yelled.

"Well?" I asked the other one.

"It's the next compartment," the man said softly, jerking his thumb toward a wall.

"Fool!" the tall man said through clenched teeth

"Okay, let's get going," I said. "To the platform. Out."

The one with the broken nose opened the door and went into the corridor, and I shoved the tall one after him. There was nobody in the corridor, so I kept the Luger out.

"Move," I ordered, jamming the gun into the tall man's ribs.

In a moment we reached the platforms between the cars. I stood well behind them and held the Luger on them. "Okay, jump," I ordered.

They gave me hard looks.

"The train is moving very fast," the broken-nosed gunman said.

"Not as fast as the slug from this gun," I warned him.

After a brief hesitation, the broken-nosed thug opened the door and jumped. In the next instant, the tall man threw himself desperately at me. I met the assault with the barrel of the Luger, smacking it hard into his midsection. He groaned and fell heavily to the metal floor at my feet, unconscious. I holstered the Luger, dragged him to the open door, and threw him off the train.

I saw his limp form hit the gravel and then bound out of sight in tall grass. He was probably better off than if he had been conscious, but either way I would not have wasted much sleep over it. After all, he had tried to blow me into little pieces.

Now there was Richter. He was on this train, and I had to find him. I was rather looking forward to it.

Thirteen

There was little choice left. The train would be nearing Dimitrovgrad and entering Bulgaria soon, and then my job would get much tougher. I could not just sit back and wait for Richter to show himself. I had to make a methodical search of the sleeping compartments, knocking on each and every door. The tactic might get me in trouble with the porter, but I had to chance that.

I decided to go to the far end of the first sleeping car, the one toward the front of the train. I would start my search at its far end and work my way back through both cars. But that plan became suddenly and dramatically unnecessary. As I reached a point about halfway through the first sleeping car, a compartment door opened, and there was Hans Richter in the corridor just a few feet from me, staring at me as if I were an apparition.

"You!" he hissed.

I noticed that he was carrying the radio.

"Call it quits, Richter," I warned. "You're not making it to Sofia now."

But Richter had other ideas. He uttered something under his breath in German, then he whirled and started running down the corridor away from me.

He was heading toward the sleeping car I had just left, toward the end of the train. The train was too crowded to attempt a shot. Instead I gave chase.

A couple of moments later Richter was on the rear platform of the train. He had gone as far as he could go in that direction. When I got to the door, Wilhelmina out, he was waiting for me. The door slammed back against me as I tried to move through its opening on the platform. I almost lost my footing as the door struck my chest and arm. Richter had given it a hard shove. I stepped warily through the doorway and just got a glimpse of Richter disappearing up a ladder that led to the top of the car.

"Give up, Richter!" I shouted above the noise of the train. But he had disappeared from view.

There seemed little to do but follow him.

I leaned out over the tracks, looking up the ladder, and just in time I saw Richter aiming at my head with a small Belgian revolver. The gun barked out, I ducked back, and the slug spent itself on the speeding ground under the wheels. Then Richter was moving along the top of the car toward the front of the train.

I swung quickly onto the ladder and climbed it to the top of the car. Richter was already at the far end, leaping from the dining car to the last sleeper. He lost his balance momentarily, as he landed on the top of the next car, but he kept his footing.

I ran along the top of the dining car after him. When I reached the end of it, I leaped the distance between it and the sleeper without pausing and kept running.

Richter turned and fired two more shots at me. I saw him aim and ducked low. Both shots went wild, although the second one chewed at the car roof under my feet. I returned fire with Wilhelmina, but with the train moving under us, my aim was bad, too, and the slug sang harmlessly past Richter's head. Then he was running again.

Richter jumped another space between cars. He was getting better at it. I followed; we ran and leaped the length of several more cars. Richter was now getting close to the front of the train.

As Richter made another jump between cars, the train swerved, and he fell to one knee. When he turned and saw me closing on him, he aimed the small revolver again and fired two more shots. I flattened myself on the top of the next car, and the slugs chewed up wood on the superstructure beside my head and arm. Richter pulled the trigger of the revolver a third time, but nothing happened. Then he angrily hurled the gun at me. It bounced off the car top and disappeared over the edge.

Richter was turning and running again. I rose, holstered the Luger, and followed. Then I saw a mountainside loom ahead and a black opening yawning in it—tunnel. The train rocketed into the tunnel, and Richter flattened himself just in time as his car disappeared into the blackness. I threw myself face down, too, and then I was immersed in darkness. In a moment I saw the disc of light growing at the other end, and emerged from the black tube into daylight again.

Richter was already moving toward the engine. I got to my feet and ran after him. I wanted to prevent him from getting back down to the interior of the train. He jumped onto the first day coach behind the engine and kept going. When I made the jump, the train lurched around a sharp bend in the tracks. I fell to my right and almost slipped off the top of the car.

I waited until the tracks straightened again. Then I moved on toward Richter. The train swayed again over some uneven track as Richter neared the front of the car. He fell and dropped the radio. It slid to the edge of the car roof, but Richter grabbed it before it went over.

Richter was at the front end of the car now. He was looking at the engine as I moved to close the small distance between us. He decided against jumping to the engine and moved instead to the ladder leading over the side of the car. I reached him just as he got one foot on it.

I grabbed him with all my strength and pulled

him up to the car roof. He glared at me as he struggled to break free.

"Let me go!" he yelled. "Do you think I have created all this for nothing?"

His words were almost whisked away by the wind before I could grasp what he was saying. But his eyes told me everything. I was succeeding where everybody else had failed, and Hans Richter was finally trapped. In a few short days, I had become his nemesis.

I slammed a fist into his square face and broke his nose.

Richter fell to the roof of the moving car. The countryside slipped past below us at a dizzying pace. I grabbed at him again, but he kicked out and knocked my legs from under me, and I fell beside him and rolled to the very edge of the roof.

I glanced at the rush of ground below me as I grabbed at the edge of the roof with my hands and legs. While I inched away from the edge, Richter regained his feet. Then, as I turned to rise, he kicked out at my head.

I evaded the kick, and Richter lost his balance again, and slipped to his knees. We both struggled to our feet together, but I had the edge this time. I slammed a fist into his midsection, and he doubled under the impact. Then I swung hard at the side of his head and connected. He staggered backward and almost fell down again.

I was now between Richter and the front edge

of the car's roof. With a last desperate effort, he swung the radio at my head. This time I saw it coming and side-stepped as Richter came at me. The momentum of his charge carried him past me to the end of the car and over it. As he flew by, I grabbed at the radio and snatched it from his grasp. Richter plummeted into the open space between the car and the engine.

I had no chance to save him. I almost went over myself as I grabbed at the radio. In another instant, Richter was falling between the car and the engine, and then he had hit the tracks below. In a split-second, the car rolled over his crumpled form.

It was not a pretty sight. Richter did not even have time to scream. The body disappeared under the moving car. Then as I glanced over the side, I saw a torn leg and another part of the body that was not identifiable tumble away from the track bed. The Butcher of Belgrade had been chopped up.

The train was slowing. We were obviously nearing Dimitrovgrad, and I could not be on that train when it got there. I climbed down the ladder that Richter had tried to use earlier, and as the train slowed even more, I jumped to the rushing ground.

I tried to keep my legs under me, but I could not. I turned head over heels twice, scraping flesh and tearing cloth as I rolled. Then, miraculously, I ended on my back at the bottom of a small embankment, and I saw the observation platform of the train recede down the track.

I felt for broken bones, but I found none. I had lost the radio, but that was lying within fifteen feet of me. I moved over to it, and in the light of a late afternoon sun, opened it at the back and looked inside. There it was as I had concluded, set into the works of the radio so that it looked like part of the circuitry—the satellite monitoring device.

I closed the radio as I shook my head. My left hand and cheek burned where they had been rubbed raw by gravel along the track bed. I wiped at my face with a handkerchief and looked down the track toward the place where Richter had fallen off the train. It was a good mile or so back there, and I could see nothing.

A parallel set of tracks ran about thirty yards away, and a slow train was approaching on them. It was going in the direction that I had just come from, heading toward the Dragoman Pass. Somewhere up ahead this train would switch over to the main track.

It was a big break for me, for it would get me out of this neighborhood in a hurry and in a way that I could avoid the authorities. I quickly crossed over to the other tracks. In a moment the train was moving past me, increasing its slow speed gradually. I waited until the last car, one of several second class coaches, was approaching, and then I started running as fast as I could. I grabbed at the rail of the steps on the rear platform and held on, and the train jerked my legs out from under me. A moment later I was standing on the platform with Hans Richter's radio still in my hand, watching the landscape around Dimitrovgrad slip into the distance.

In less than five minutes the train passed the spot where the Butcher had met an appropriate death. I saw what looked like a heap of old clothing lying between the tracks, but the debris was not identifiable as a person. The rest of Richter was lying somewhere along the far side of the tracks. I stared pensively at the heap for a long moment, and then it disappeared from sight.

Ursula would be unhappy that Richter had not been brought back to Bonn for trial. But there had been a kind of justice in the end of his ugly career—a kind of violent retribution.

Ursula and I would spend tonight in some small room at Crveni Krst. I would touch her body, and we would think only of those warm moments together.

We had earned the right.

Nick Carter in an unbeatable spy
adventure series

War in Tandem editions

The Battle of Britain (Illus.)   H. St. George Saunders   25p
Official records from the British and German sides and the
  recollections of the pilots themselves. The really authentic story.

Assault from Within   Georg von Konrat   35p
Six hundred young Germans trained to speak, think, eat, sleep
  and dream as Russians were infiltrated behind the enemy lines
  to cause destruction and chaos.

Rage of Battle   T. S. Hope   30p
A savage record of blood, carnage and death, as experienced by a
  sixteen-year-old infantryman.

Barry's Flying Column   Ewan Butler   25p
The story of the I.R.A.'s Cork No. 3 Brigade 1919–21.

Operation Mercury   M. G. Comeau   30p
An airman in the Battle of Crete – 'a record of heroism, of en-
  durance, and of gaiety in the most daunting circumstances.'
  Air Chief Marshal Sir Philip Joubert de la Ferte.

Marshal Without Glory   Ewan Butler and Gordon Young   40p
The life and death of Hermann Goering.

Evil Genius   Erich Ebermayer and Hans-Otto Meissner   35p
The life and death of Joseph Goebbels.

Pocket Battleship   Theodor Krancke and H. J. Brennecke   35p
The exciting account of the famous German raider, *Admiral
  Scheer*, which sank 152,000 tons of Allied shipping.

The Raider Kormoran   Captain Theodor Detmers   35p
The exploits of a German 'mystery ship' in World War II.

Stephen John

I Like It That Way

Follow the outrageous adventures of offbeat art dealer, Albert Divine. Aided and abetted throughout by his voluptuous model girl friend, Angela, he succumbs to much skulduggery in the spheres of art and bed during a meteoric rise which hurtles him into the orgiastic orbits of some pretty peculiar characters. Not for the squeamish, the humourless or the intolerant, it makes the Permissive Society seem like a Victorian vicarage tea party.

How About This Way?

Art dealer extraordinary, Albert Divine, is on the rampage again. This time, in the freaky world of the weird and beautiful people on the Riviera, he is overcome in turn by the sun, the liquor, and a variety of lustful ladies. His host's totally original hobby of re-enacting scenes from great paintings, embellished by what the artist dared not paint, involves Albert with an enthusiastic group of tourists who finally let down their bikinis for a re-staging of that masterpiece, the *Rape of the Sabines*.

Any Way You Like

An all-expenses-paid trip in search of ithy-phallic statuettes and virility fetishes takes Albert to Africa. There he rubs more than shoulders with the accomplished explorer Gloria Eisenway whose book *Getting It Up In Africa* involves some amazing research. Angela, too, finds the climate stimulating, and discovers a new outlet for her talents playing a leading role in a tribal fertility rite.

and

This Way, Please!

'*How Albert manages to keep it up I shall never know.*'
Ariadne, Amanda, Angela, Jane, Lavinia, Alison. . . .

Name ....

Address ....

Titles required.....................................

....

....

....

....

....

....

....

The publishers hope that you enjoyed this book and invite you to write for the full list of Tandem titles.

If you find any difficulty in obtaining these books from your usual retailer we shall be pleased to supply the titles of your choice upon receipt of your remittance.

Packing and postage charges are as follows:
1 book – 7p per copy, 2-4 books – 5p per copy, 5-8 books – 4p per copy.

WRITE NOW TO:
Universal-Tandem Publishing Co. Ltd.
14 Gloucester Road,
London SW7 4RD